Summer
Soldiers

SUMMER SOLDIERS

♦

SUSAN HART LINDQUIST

Delacorte Press

Published by
Delacorte Press
a division of Random House, Inc.
1540 Broadway
New York, New York 10036

Library of Congress Cataloging-in-Publication Data

Lindquist, Susan Hart.
    Summer soldiers / Susan Hart Lindquist.
        p.   cm.
    Summary: After his father goes off to war during the summer of 1918, eleven-year-old Joe, along with his friends, contends with the town bullies and tries to figure out the meaning of courage.
    ISBN 0-385-32641-6
    [1. Fathers and sons—Fiction.   2. World War, 1914–1918—Fiction.   3. Bullies—Fiction.   4. Courage—Fiction.]   I. Title.
PZ7.L6593Su   1999
[Fic]—dc21   98-47429
                                                              CIP
                                                               AC

The text of this book is set in 12.25-point Minion.

Book design by Semadar Megged

Manufactured in the United States of America

June 1999

10   9   8   7   6   5   4   3   2   1

BVG

FOR MY PARENTS

AND FOR MGMFB

AND HERS

ONLY WHEN WE RESPECT A MAN'S RIGHT TO CHOOSE
DO WE TRULY RESPECT HIS FREEDOM.

CHAPTER **I**

SURE THING, IT WASN'T US who caused the trouble. Nobody could have said we were doing anything but minding our own business, Jim and Luther and Billy and me—just sitting peaceful on that fence, kicking our boots against the rail and waiting to be called over to the picnic tables for dinner.

The long, hot, dusty day was finally rolling on into twilight, that red August sun hanging lazy in the treetops across the river. We were all enjoying the way the breeze from the ocean was coming up behind us over Morgan's horse pasture, cooling our sunburned necks.

The four of us were just relaxing and congratulating ourselves for the hard work we'd put in helping our daddies on the sheep drive, when right out of nowhere a soggy old horse apple came zooming through the air and hit Luther splat on the forehead.

We all leaped off that fence quick as hop-toads.

"It's them," Jim Morgan said, crouching low as another manure rocket whizzed by. "It's Harley and those other two lousy brothers of yours, Luther."

"Who else *would* it be?" Luther said. "They've been waiting all day for a chance to get us."

Up till then it had been a fine day. In fact, it had been a regular celebration of wild times. We'd worked hard, whooping those sheep over the hill to Maxwell like regular drovers, them flowing along easy as water without straying off even once. And there'd been no trouble with Luther's brothers since we'd taken care to keep our daddies between us and them.

Yep, it had been a fine time all around. No trouble with the Thornton boys, no trouble with the sheep. We'd gotten a good price for our lambs, and for a change there'd been no talk of the war.

I looked over at Luther. A big green splot of manure was dripping down the side of his face. I couldn't help but laugh.

"What you grinning at, Joe?" He whacked me on the arm, then wiped his cheek with his sleeve. "You don't look so pretty yourself." Sure enough, I'd taken a hit on my shoulder.

Another volley of manure bombs came hurtling our way. Billy ducked, checking the back of his shirt. He made a good target with all that red hair of his. "Where are they? You see them?"

We peered through the fence rails.

"There!" Jim said, pointing toward the big cotton-wood tree out in the pasture.

All three of Luther's big brothers—Harley and Ray and Arlo—came strolling out from behind the tree, innocent as newborn lambs, acting as if they hadn't done a thing.

Sure there were four of us and only three of them, but they were older and more muscled up than any of us eleven-year-olds. Luther's oldest brother, Harley, was sixteen and built like he'd been a lumberjack all his life. Ray was short but bulldog mean, and Arlo was near as mean, just maybe not as quick and smart. But *we* were smart. Smart enough to know not to take them on.

"We could make a run for it," Billy said.

I guess we could have. Our mamas were there just across the yard setting dinner out on the tables, and our daddies were there too, talking by the fire. If we could get to them we'd be safe.

But that patch of ground between us and our parents might as well have been that bloody battlefield called no-man's-land way over there in Europe.

"Here they come," said Billy, backing up against the fence.

They were passing through the gate and walking around to our side.

"Whoa, now!" Harley said, stopping to point at us. "Look there! It's the Hobby Horse Gang. Looks like they've been riding the wrong end of their horses."

"That Harley's a bigger bully than the German Kaiser," Billy mumbled, soft, so none of them could hear.

Might not have been quite *that* bad, but I swear, no group of boys ever had a stronger talent for tormentation.

All three of them busted up laughing at the sight of

us, hunkered down there by the fence all decorated and stunk up with manure.

Right then I figured it sure would have been nice if all those boys were old enough to get drafted. Maybe somebody'd even send them over to France so they could get themselves shot by those Germans.

"Ha!" said Ray. "Look there at Luther. Looks like little brother and his friends messed themselves!"

"I'm telling you!" Harley said, taking a wide step around us, sniffing the air. "Smells like it too!"

"Ah, they stink, all right," said Ray. "Just as bad as usual!"

"You tykes need a good wash," Arlo said.

"Naw," said Harley. "Leave 'em be. The flies'll clean them off. Come on, let's go get some food."

The three of them started off across the grass toward the picnic area.

Now, I'm of the mind that things might have died down after that, if Luther had stayed put. But that wasn't Luther's way. I guess he decided he'd had enough. He stood up and started after them.

I yanked on his pant leg. "Stay down," I said. "Stay down and they'll leave us alone."

But Luther didn't listen. He pulled away and headed straight out across the yard.

"Hey!" he yelled.

Ever since we were big enough to matter to Harley and those boys, Jim and Billy and I'd done our best to steer clear of them—just to avoid losing any blood. But not Luther. Once he got going, he'd egg his three big brothers on with his sassy mouth just like he *wanted* to get kicked around.

"We going to stop him?" Billy asked, looking over at me. Trail dirt had dusted out all his freckles, but I could still see worry in his eyes.

Jim looked sort of worried too.

"Face-to-face!" Luther shouted at his brothers again, making his hands into fists. He was getting way too excited. "Any one of you! Face-to-face!"

Billy and Jim gave me that worried look again.

"Hey, Luther!" I shouted at him.

"Come on, Luther," Billy said. "Knock it off. You're going to get us all killed."

Luther just grinned back at us. Then he did an about-face, cupped his hands around his mouth, and shouted, "What are you, Harley? Chicken or something?"

Like they were lined up ready to do a dance together, those big Thornton boys turned all three at the same time.

Jim looked at me. I looked at Jim. Billy said, "Uh-oh"; then the three of us scrambled over the fence.

"We'll see who's chicken!" Harley called back, coming fast across the field.

Quick as that, those boys had a hold on Luther. Even quicker they dragged him over the grass and dunked him headfirst in the watering trough.

That's about the time Luther's daddy finally noticed what was going on. He came charging across the yard like a bee-stung bull.

"Quit!" Mr. Thornton shouted, grabbing Ray and Arlo by the back of their shirts. He yelled at Harley to leave Luther and the rest of us alone. "You get to that table and help your mama!" His face had gone hot poker red and he looked angry enough to chew bullets. Arlo was the only one slow enough to get a hard kick in the rear end with Mr. Thornton's boot.

Considering that boot and his daddy's expression, Luther could have done a whole lot more thinking just then. He would have been smart to hold his tongue. But as usual, he spoke up like no one else was around. "Yeah, you stupid hens!" he yelled at his brothers. "Go help Mama!"

Luther's daddy came swooping down on him like a hawk and shook him so hard water came flying out of his ears. "*You* button that lip, mister, or you'll get worse from me than they *ever* gave you!" Mr. Thornton plopped Luther down hard on the ground, then left him there and stomped off, so mad you could practically see steam rising from his head.

Papa and the other men joined us then, and we climbed back over the fence.

Jim's daddy gave Luther a hand up off the ground. "You all right, son?"

"Sure, Mr. Morgan. I'm okay."

"You too, Jim?" his daddy asked.

"I'm all right, Pa. We're all fine."

"I wonder what comes over those boys," Papa said as he brushed off my sleeve.

Mr. Teale nodded, dampening his handkerchief in the trough and wiping Billy's face.

Papa shook his head. "I wonder why they can't seem to leave you boys alone."

Papa wondered about everything. He spoke that way, all the time starting sentences with, "I wonder . . . ," then ending with something like ". . . what the moon is made of" or ". . . why the sky is blue" or ". . . why they can't seem to leave you boys alone."

"I don't know," I said. "I wonder about that too."

"They're not so tough," Luther said, pretending as usual that he could have handled them.

If I'd spoken for myself I'd have said I was mighty glad our daddies showed up to keep those Thornton boys from licking us as good as I knew they could. Just like the French and those other folks in Europe were probably saying hearty thanks to us for helping to save them from the Germans.

NEARLY ALL THE DAYLIGHT was gone, and across the yard bugs were coming up around the lanterns on the tables.

Papa and I walked over to join Mama and the others. I tried to slick back my hair when I saw Jim's sister, Claire, walking across the grass carrying a platter of biscuits. She was dressed up clean and fresh as a meadow. My little sisters, Alice and Helen, were tagging along after her. Their voices came floating over the pasture with the sound of waking crickets.

"It's been a long day, Joe," Papa said, laying his hand on my shoulder. "Let's try to keep the peace."

"I'll do my best," I said.

Our mamas took care of that—sat us with Alice and Helen at a different table from Luther's brothers—so we kept the peace pretty easy during dinner. More so than our daddies, that's a sure thing. Straightaway they got to talking about the war, same as they'd been doing for the last three years, ever since 1914 when it began.

But I have to say, I didn't blame them. It was all mighty exciting. Heck, soon as President Wilson finally got us into the war last April, you couldn't take two steps down Main Street without seeing a flag, or a billboard shouting out "Buy War Bonds!" or "Enlist!" Sometimes Luther and Jim and Billy and I would get to talking about maybe going over there too, to fight like the heroes from the war biographies we'd been made to read in school—stories about the brave lives of George Washington and Joan of Arc. We talked big about being ace bomber pilots or doughboys charging out of those trenches and crossing into no-man's-land to take on the German army.

Our daddies talked big too, and they were stirring up some commotion at their table, all their voices blending into one, getting riled about the war.

"I'd like to give those lousy Huns a piece of my mind!"

"Ought to join up and go after that Kaiser Wilhelm ourselves!"

"You bet! That coward'd be no match for us!"

"Sure enough. We'd finish up over there and be back home by Christmas!"

Luther's daddy was getting so agitated that he had to

get up and start pacing around the table, kicking up dust with his boots.

"Hell, yes!" he said. "No disputing we've waited long enough!"

Right then Mrs. Thornton pulled him back down into his seat and the rest of the women set into changing the subject of conversation.

AFTER DINNER WE ALL SAT around the fire—all of us but those big Thornton boys. They just sort of stayed lurking at the edges of the circle like a nervous pack of wolves.

Our dog, Spit, came sidling up to Papa and lay down across his knee so he could pick the ticks out of her fur. Papa looked across the fire to where I was sitting with the fellows.

"You boys did fine today," he said. "Put in a good day's work."

"It was a fine day all around," I said, nodding. "We'll do it again next year, won't we?"

"Sheep have to get to market. Sure enough we'll be counting on all you boys to help. You and the dogs," he said, ruffling Spit's fur. She rolled over and let him scratch her stomach.

Spit had worked hard alongside the Thornton dogs, Ben and Pete. Between our four families we only had those three. The Teales never had a dog because Billy's mama said they made her sneeze. The Morgans used to have one until last spring, when she got herself kicked in the head by Mr. Morgan's best mare.

I looked over at Jim's daddy and remembered how he'd walked away after that pup died, cradling the poor thing like she was a newborn baby, blood spilling out the side of her mouth and all over Mr. Morgan's arm. Jim told me his daddy'd said later that he'd never own another dog as long as he had horses, even if it made him dependent on the rest of us when it came to working the sheep. I was glad of that, though. Kept our families together so we could have good times like these.

I went back to enjoying the evening, lazing by the fire.

Mr. Teale unpacked his guitar and we sang for a while, "Foggy, Foggy Dew" and "Red River Valley" being the only ones the boys and I really pitched in on. After that, Papa offered to give a recitation like he did every year after the drive. As a closing to the day, he said. Mama chose to hear Longfellow's "The Village Blacksmith," which I liked a whole lot better coming from Papa than I had when I read it in school.

When he finished, everyone was quiet until Mr. Teale stood up and tossed another log on the fire. " 'Thus at the flaming forge of life,' " he said, repeating a line of the poem, " 'our fortunes must be wrought . . .' "

Mr. Thornton sat forward and poked the fire with a stick. "No good fortune in that war," he said. "It's a sorry life they're living over there." Sparks crackled into the night sky.

"Too many wounded," said Papa, leaning to one side to take his knife out of his pocket. "Too many dead.

Too many starving children." When he picked up a stick to start whittling, I knew he was doing some serious thinking. "It's so difficult to understand," he said.

He was right. Everything about the war was hard to understand. Sure, I'd learned that America was fighting to save Democracy and to keep the German soldiers from coming over here, but it still didn't make much sense to me.

"Can't deny those Brits could use a bigger hand," Billy's daddy said.

Papa turned to Mr. Morgan. "What do you think, George?"

"Can't say as I know," he said. "It's all so blasted confusing." He stood up then, and walked away from the fire.

"Where's your daddy going?" I asked Jim.

"Ah, you know Pa. He's probably going out to check on the horses."

That would be like Mr. Morgan. Jim's daddy spent all the time he could with his horses—more than with human beings, I imagine.

"It's time we talked about it," Luther's daddy said.

"Maybe it's time we did more than talk," said Mr. Teale.

Mr. Thornton reached to stir the fire again.

Papa was whittling on, slowly, carefully.

"Probably our duty," Mr. Teale said.

"Yes," said Papa. "Perhaps. Perhaps it *is* the right thing to do."

Jim's mama looked across the fire toward us boys. In the firelight I saw her eyes turn, catching hold of

Mama. I looked at my mother. Her eyes were holding just as hard back on Mrs. Morgan.

Till that moment it had never occurred to me our daddies would really decide to go off and fight in the war. Never once, in fact. With wives and kids and being married so long, every single one of them was exempt from the service. None of them got drafted like what was happening to all the younger fellows in town.

I'd heard a million times that women and children were being burned and murdered in their houses over there. Heard it so many times I could recite it in my sleep. Heard that the Belgians were starving. That if we didn't help, the world would come to ruin.

Still, before that night, I never imagined my papa going—actually signing up to meet those Germans face-to-face. But he did.

CHAPTER 2

BY MORNING, ALL OUR DADDIES had decided to enlist. All of them except Jim's. Mr. Morgan said he wouldn't be going. Said his heart just wasn't in the fight. He didn't need to be a hero, he said.

I don't know if being a hero was what Papa had in mind. If it was, he sure never said so to me. Heck, for the days before he left all he talked about was some box he'd lost. He went around wondering and worrying about it, taking me aside to ask if I'd seen it.

"An old cookie tin," he said, "with a blue willow pattern. It's one my daddy gave me to keep special things in. Sharing a room with those brothers of mine, all the privacy I ever had in the world fit inside that box."

I didn't have the slightest idea why he thought finding it was so important, but wondering about it occupied his mind clear up till the night before he went away.

That evening he and I went out to walk off the big

dinner of fricassee and biscuits Mama'd made special since he was leaving. We turned up our collars and headed out toward the place where we liked to sit and talk—the ridge above our house where an old grove of cypress trees leaned against the wind. It was an especially nice spot, a flat piece of ground with a view of the valley clear to the ocean, and with two decently comfortable rocks for us to sit on.

Papa whistled for Spit to join us. She didn't like me much, but I felt sort of sorry for her anyhow. Papa was the only human on earth she cared one whit about, and she didn't even know he was leaving. She trotted along just like it was any other after-dinner walk.

We hiked up the hill without talking, but when Papa stopped to gaze out over the valley, something told me that old box was still sitting as heavy on his mind as Mama's biscuits were on our stomachs.

"Wonder if I buried it somewhere," he said.

He bent to pick a stick up off the ground before he sat down. Then he took out his jackknife. I watched the way he opened that knife, his barbed-wire-scarred fingers carefully pulling back the blade, then turning it to make it bear down on the rough bark of the stick. He curled off a clean white ribbon of wood, let it fall, then brought the blade back to pull off another, then another. Spit went scooting after the whittling chips as they scattered in the wind.

"What's so special about that box?" I asked. "What's inside?"

For just a moment, he glanced over at me. The somber look in his eyes gave me a shiver, made me remember he was leaving, and that this evening was the last I'd have with him until he came back home.

But I wasn't about to blurt out how much I'd miss him, any more than he'd be saying that to me. We talked away from how we were feeling, always skipping right over the serious stuff—sort of the way a rock can skip over water, barely touching the surface, then lifting off, light and easy—moving on to joke and wonder about something else.

So while Spit sniffed for field mice in the grass, we went on talking about that box. I asked him again what was inside.

"Who knows? Probably just toenail clippings and bent-up old fishhooks. Maybe a few prune pits . . ."

I gave him a jab in the arm. "Quit teasing," I said. "I want to know."

"Well," he said, looking thoughtful, "I believe I stowed some of Great-aunt Binny's nerve tablets away in there."

He dodged my swing.

"Yes, indeed," he said. "I'm sure I did."

Pretty soon we struck up laughing so hard we nearly fell off the rocks we were sitting on. He jumped up and ran; then we went slipping and sliding down the hill, chasing, laughing, out of breath, Spit running along with us across the back garden, through the gate, bursting into the kitchen, where Mama and the girls were washing dishes.

Mama tried to work up a frown as she reached for a dish towel and walked over to close the door behind us. It was getting dark out. She stopped to switch on the electric lights, then came by and gave Papa a swat with the towel.

He swung around, scooped her up into his arms, and kissed her right there in front of us in the middle of the kitchen.

Helen giggled. I guess five is too young to be embarrassed by something like that. But Alice was nine and just stood across the room fiddling with the knob on the cooler door, looking nervous and uncomfortable. I took time to examine a crack in the ceiling.

When they finally finished, Papa sat down at the table, Mama poured him a cup of hot coffee, and then both girls rushed him like he was a big old piece of apple pie.

"When are you coming home, Papa?" Alice asked.

"In the blink of an eye, little one," he said. "You'll see. I'll be home before Christmas."

"Did you speak to George Morgan?" asked Mama.

Aside from driving stock to market, there are a few other big things to be taken care of when you raise sheep for a living: like lambing, and marking, and of course, shearing. Manpower is important in these matters. That's why all four of our families—the Morgans, the Teales, the Thorntons, and us Farringtons—always did the big work together. For as long as I could remember our daddies had helped each other.

"It's all arranged," Papa said. "He'll be in charge while we're gone. Won't be long. And the Thornton boys will give him a hand. Harley's sixteen now. He knows sheep. I'm trusting they'll do a fine job looking after things."

A fine job? Mr. Morgan surely would, but Luther's big brothers would probably only do a fine job of tormenting the rest of us. I was about to speak my mind on this matter, but just then Helen jumped into Papa's lap and poked him with her finger.

"I have a splinter, Papa. See?" she said.

He looked at it, then motioned to me. "Come here, Joe. Time you took this job over for me." He pulled out that knife of his and put it into my hand. It felt heavy and was still warm from him holding it. "You know how it's done. Be gentle, that's all. Slip the tip of the blade nice and easy, then give a little pull."

"No!" Helen hollered so loud you'd have thought Papa'd just told me to cut out her eyeballs. "You, Papa! I want *you* to do it. Don't let Joe! It'll hurt if he does it!"

Her bottom lip was starting to do that quiver dance it does just before she starts bawling. Mama came over and put her hand on Papa's shoulder. "Maybe *you* ought to do it, Russell. It won't pay to get anyone upset. Not tonight."

Papa sighed; then I sighed to keep him company; then I gave him the knife so he could take out my sister's splinter and keep everyone happy.

I THINK THE DOWNSTAIRS CLOCK chiming five was what woke me, or maybe that first bit of daylight peeking through my curtain. I rolled away from it, listening.

A motor rumbled.

I hauled myself out of bed and hurried to the window, just in time to see Papa and the others drive off in the Thorntons' car. I watched them make their way toward the end of the valley, watched them till they disappeared up over the hill.

I stood there for a long time, staring out at the empty road. I could hear Mama downstairs in the kitchen. The house sounded normal, and felt right for a late-September morning. Cool, airy. I pulled on my clothes and was ready to go down to see her, when I noticed Papa's jackknife on the table by my bed.

Till that split second, I guess I figured life around the house would be pretty much the same as always. He'd just not be there was all. But his knife lying there told me different—told me some of what Papa had not said, some of the serious stuff he'd skipped over last night. Be brave, like him. Be strong. Make him proud. He was trusting me to stand in his stead.

I clearly didn't know if I was ready for that.

CHAPTER 3

READY OR NOT, THERE I WAS—me, Joseph Michael Farrington, all of eleven years old and overnight the boss of the family, charged with looking after my sweet tired mama and my two silly little sisters.

None of my friends had it quite so bad. Sure, Luther's brothers were gone most of the time, boarding at Mrs. Tilley's sister's house over in Maxwell so they could get a high-school education, but they came home some weekends to help Mrs. Thornton and work the sheep. As for Billy, he didn't mind helping his mama—he was used to it, being the only child of Mr. and Mrs. Teale. And of course, Jim Morgan's life didn't change at all—or at least not right away.

I picked up quick on doing the manly chores like the hard lifting around the house. I beat the carpets, turned the mattresses, chopped and stacked the wood. And every day I had to load the kitchen woodbox and prime the pump if that needed to be done; then Mama would send me out to rake leaves, sweep the walk, or ditch the garden. On Tuesdays I'd offer help to Mr. Twining, who delivered the ice. On Saturdays I'd burn the rubbish in the metal drum out back.

It was all hard work, but harder still was seeing that downhearted expression Mama wore for the first few weeks after Papa went away. Sometimes it would be just the two of us reading in the living room at the end of the day, the girls tucked in and asleep upstairs, the house so quiet it made the clock ticking on the mantel sound loud as a hammer. Mama'd get up from her chair, walk to the mantel, and touch the picture of Papa—the one of him in his new uniform. She'd turn to gaze at me, her eyes looking lost and sad, that clock ticking away, and she'd say, "Well, Joe. I guess it's the end of another day."

I'd want to say, "I wonder when Papa will be home," because that's what her eyes were asking. They'd make me start missing Papa so bad I'd have to turn away or leap out of my chair and run to bed. Not one bit brave or manly in the least.

But before we knew it, the weeks rolled away into months, and I got sort of used to living without Papa—used to being the man of the house.

During those months we followed the war-doings on maps cut from the Sunday paper that we stuck up on the kitchen wall with pushpins. We bought Liberty Bonds to support the war effort, donated books for soldiers to read, and twice a week Mama volunteered over at the Red Cross in Maxwell.

But over that time I never tried to take out any splinters for the girls. Once or twice I used Papa's knife to cut twine or slice jerky. And I whittled some. But always in private, not wanting particularly to share the fact that Papa'd given his knife to me. Somehow, I didn't feel like I'd earned it, simply by his going to war. So I mostly just carried it around, letting it be heavy in my pocket as a reminder of him.

It was clear to me that Papa'd left me in charge of his knife. And just as clear he'd left Mr. Morgan in charge of the sheep, like he'd said. Unfortunately, I don't think he made that point quite clear enough to Harley Thornton.

From the beginning Harley thought he was a big shot because his daddy'd given him charge of their dogs, Ben and Pete. Ben was a collie, a good reliable sheep dog who'd had lots of practice. Pete was young, but he could round up a wayward ewe fast as lightning. Lots better than our dog, Spit, who wouldn't mind anybody once Papa'd left. So there we were, all of us dependent on Harley and those dogs, while he yelled at them, at his brothers, at us, and sometimes even at Mr. Morgan.

Despite that, we made it through lambing season and on into spring, with Mr. Morgan standing by to even things out in his gentle way, trying to keep the peace.

Sometimes, after the fellows and I'd had supper at Jim's because we'd played late or helped his mama shoo the goats out of her yard, Mr. Morgan would sit down to visit with us on the front steps. He wouldn't say anything at first; he'd just take out his pipe, pull a bag of Prince Albert out of his pants pocket, and shove his pipe full. Believe me, there was no smell in the world sweeter than that pipe tobacco he smoked those evenings on the porch. He'd tamp it down with his thumb, scrape a match along the porch step, then take quick short draws on the pipe till it lit.

He might see something off on the horizon, or get a thought, or have an old horse story to tell, and off he'd go on an easy, rambling journey into another place in his head, his soft words taking us right along.

Maybe Mr. Morgan's gentleness was the reason none of us were too surprised when he didn't go to war. Somehow it was hard to picture him tossing a grenade or stabbing anyone with a bayonet—even a German. Besides, even if some folks said he should have gone off with the rest of them, it was nice just knowing one of our daddies was still around.

PAPA WROTE TO US at least once a week, all about his doings in camp; about how he'd learned to adjust a gas mask and how he'd helped a fellow or two learn to cut barbed wire. The army had him taking French lessons so he'd know how to ask for help if he lost his way in France, and they taught him personal hygiene and proper care of his feet. Not exactly entertaining reading, but it was nice to hear from him just the same.

According to Luther, his daddy mostly wrote about wanting to hurry up and get over to France so he could start killing Germans. Billy's daddy, who'd joined the American Field Service, had already been sent to France to drive an ambulance, so for months, we'd been hearing about the mangled and shot-up and blown-apart bodies Mr. Teale had to pull out of the mud over there. It wasn't that I wanted to hear stuff like that from Papa, but news about something besides his feet might have been nice.

We wrote back to him, of course, the girls in pencil, me in pen and ink, all of us around the big oak table, making sure not to write discouraging things, making sure to tell him that we were all being brave, and that we were getting along fine without him.

Which we were, I guess. Until sometime in April when Papa and Mr. Thornton finally got shipped over to France.

Papa went over with thousands of other soldiers. We were in the thick of the war now, and every day more and more of our fellows were being reported missing or killed.

As it got worse over there in Europe, it got worse over here too. Folks began to worry about spies and foreigners, and more of them spoke up in earnest about hating those Devil Huns. Flags started waving higher, billboards started shouting louder, and folks started pointing out Mr. Morgan as a slacker who was afraid to fight in the war.

Harley picked right up on it, and it didn't take long before he made the big announcement that he wasn't going to let Mr. Morgan take charge of the sheep any longer.

We'd been working up on the hill, all of us helping to string a new line of fence, Harley grumbling whenever Mr. Morgan tried to give him advice. We were almost done, loading up wire and posts and such in the wagon, when Harley marched up and tapped Mr. Morgan on the shoulder.

"Now that school's near finished," he said, "we'll all do just fine running the show without you. Don't want to have to count on a slacker to help us get our work done."

Mr. Morgan didn't protest. He just walked away, stooping to pull a length of grass to chew on, then heading out across the field alone.

That was when I started wondering if we'd make it without Papa. I knew it could only get worse. Once school let out, Luther's brothers would be back on our side of the hill for the whole summer. And we boys knew that the torment they'd dish out would be meaner than ever. What with them feeling so strongly patriotic now, we knew they'd give *all* of us hell every chance they got just because we hung around with Jim.

CHAPTER 4

BUT THORNTON BOYS or no Thornton boys, we still planned to have a good summer.

Over the winter and through spring, Luther and Jim and Billy and I had spent most of our free time hanging around at Billy's because he had a rumpus room with toys galore—everything from an Erector set to a Mechanical Aeroplane with a real whirling propeller.

It was good fun, but now we had the whole valley as our playroom. So every day after chores, and Sundays after church, we planned to hightail it outdoors as quick as we could.

"Let's hobble Mrs. Hicks's old cow," Billy might suggest.

"Or we could climb the bell tower and paint it red," Luther'd say, ready to do most anything on a dare.

"A fox was screaming outside my house last night," Jim would offer. "Let's go out and bag it."

What we ended up doing wasn't usually so dramatic. We'd talk big about having wild adventures or we'd carry on deep contemplation about becoming master criminals, but mostly we just hung around at the river or hid out in the Pepperwood Grove.

The Pepperwood Grove was a dark, shady, secret place, tucked away off the road. It was our territory and had been since we were about five or six years old.

We used to pretend to hunt treasure there, and we'd play king of the mountain, knocking each other off tree stumps and fallen logs. Nowadays we played war games, if we played at all. Usually we'd just laze around swapping jokes and telling whoppers.

It was a great place to pass time, but that first day of vacation the only thing we wanted to do was fish. All of us had found willow sticks for poles and we'd stripped them smooth and outfitted them with wrapping twine and hooks. Soon as chores were done we planned to try them out.

I was just heading outside to meet Luther, when Mama corralled me and stood me on a chair so I could model a dress she was sewing as a present for Great-aunt Binny. Turned out the Thornton boys were not the only ones expected in town. Aunt Binny and Uncle Chester were set to arrive from San Francisco toward the end of the week.

"Their neighbors have opened their house as a stay-over for men on leave," Mama explained. "Binny says the soldiers' comings and goings keep her awake at night, so I went ahead and invited them both to come to us. She seems to think I need her help anyway."

I couldn't imagine Binny being much help to anyone, but I guess Mama felt sorry for her. And I suppose I must have too, otherwise I wouldn't have been standing there silly as anything in that flowered dress, with a pillow tied to my backside and a sofa cushion to my front. It seemed doubtful that this was what Papa imagined I'd be doing as the man of the house after he went away.

Spit got so nervous when she saw me that she went scurrying to the kitchen. At least the girls were out back hanging wash, so they weren't there to rib me.

But then Luther showed up.

Like always, he walked in the back door without knocking. When he came strolling into the living room and saw me, he nearly fell over and died.

"What are you grinning at?" I asked, wiggling away from Mama and her pins.

Luther doubled over and laughed so hard he had to sit down. Mama finally sent him back into the kitchen for a cup of water while she unharnessed me from those cushions. She let me skedaddle after that.

Luther was still whooping and hee-hawing when we got outside on the street. I figure it was his fault that our neighbor Mrs. Marble looked up from her gardening and shook her head in disapproval. We had to smile and wave back, though, just to be nice. Everyone was nice to Mrs. Marble, no matter how disagreeable she was.

Her son, Andy, died last winter on the Western Front. Everyone said he was a real hero, enlisting with the British months before President Wilson declared war, and making the ultimate sacrifice. Saying Andy Marble's name was like waving a flag, and you could hear folks talking about him under their breath whenever Jim's daddy walked by.

"So why the dress?" Luther finally asked when he'd stopped laughing.

"It's for Great-aunt Binny. She's coming for a visit. Says Mama needs the help. She thinks the girls and I are *so* much trouble."

Luther patted my back in sympathy. "That's a real shame. I'd have you stay over at my place, but tell the truth, I'd take Binny any day over what I've got living with me. They're home, you know." Luther stopped and rolled up his sleeve. A big round purple bruise was blooming just above his elbow. "They did me over once already and they've only been home a day," he said. "Ray's the only one who got me, though. Only socked me once before I scared him off."

"Sure thing. You bet," I said, not believing him for a second. I took a quick look around. "Where are they?"

"They went up to fix fence on the hill this morning." He glanced over his shoulder. "They're probably back by now. Out there somewhere. Looking for us." He rolled his sleeve down and gave me a little push forward. "Let's get out of here."

When we got to Billy's he was sitting on the steps of his porch, scooting his Friction Auto Racer back and forth beside him, looking bored as anything.

"Hey there!" he said, leaping to his feet when he saw us. "I've been waiting hours. It's taken you so long, that lousy river started running backwards." He grabbed his fishing pole and went zooming off ahead of us flying an imaginary airplane.

Billy was always imagining crazy stuff. A couple of years ago he thought he was Pancho Villa. Last spring he was Ty Cobb, driving us all to distraction, stopping to practice hitting invisible baseballs while we were walking around town. Now all he wanted to be was that famous ace pilot Major Billy Bishop. He'd taken to buzzing around in circles like a perfect idiot whenever the mood struck him. Queer, honestly, since he'd never even seen a real airplane.

We followed him past the new schoolhouse—new maybe, but still so small that any kids who went on to high school had to board over in Maxwell at Mrs. Tilley's sister's house. Not even Luther's brothers complained about that, though; both she and Mrs. Tilley were champion cooks. Their strawberry rhubarb pie had won the county fair's highest pie honor for six years straight.

After we passed the schoolhouse and the library, Billy pulled around beside us and we started up Main Street, having to cross through town to get to Jim's.

Main Street was the most patriotic place in town, red, white, and blue with flags, and plastered with billboards to remind everyone to buy war bonds and Liberty Stamps.

We counted automobiles as we went. There were lots of them around town now.

Papa bought his first car back in 1916. It was a

Model T. Nice, of course, but not as quick as the Hudson we had now, and not half as big and grand.

We counted twelve cars by the time we reached Hicks's Feedstore.

Like always, Mr. Peck and Mr. Lyle were sitting out front in the sun when we went by.

"Howdy, boys," Mr. Lyle said. "You see this?" He waved his hand toward the newspaper Mr. Peck was holding.

Mr. Peck nodded to us and held up his paper, pointing with his own bony finger to yesterday's headline and shouting, "Says here, 'Austrian Armies Crushed on Piave.' Says they're making a 'disordered retreat!' Looks like your pappies are doing a fine and dandy job over there!"

The three of us stuck out our chests, feeling proud as all get-out, knowing our fathers were fighting hard to bring victory to the Allies—even though I was pretty sure Papa wasn't anywhere near Italy, and could hardly say I knew what job he was really doing over there.

We turned the corner in front of Jepson's Grocery, passing by the poster of the soldier that had been hanging in the window for more than a year.

I'd been with Papa the first day they put that thing up. He'd brought me uptown to buy a roll of Necco wafers because I'd earned a nickel shoveling gravel for our new driveway. We stood in front of the poster for a long, long time, me feeling small looking up at the handsome man in uniform, Papa standing behind me, his big hands resting on my shoulders. He never said so, but I figure maybe that poster helped him decide to go off and fight in the war.

Luther clapped me on the back. "Move along, Joe! You in a trance, or something? Jim's waiting."

IT WAS A WALK to Jim's house. He lived a far bit up the river on the other side of the bridge, on the ranch that had belonged to his grandfather. It was a beat-up sort of run-down place that still had an outhouse instead of an indoor toilet. And it didn't have a telephone or electricity either, since the poles hadn't been strung that far past town yet.

When we got there his mama was out hanging wash with his sister, Claire. I stood back by the front gate, watching Claire from a distance, the way I always did because her good looks made me so nervous.

"Jimmy's out back with Daddy," she said, her voice smoothing over the yard, then over me, like honey. "With the horses."

"No surprise," Luther said, smiling at her.

Luther was right. Jim's daddy was always with the horses, always with his hand on one, or talking to one, or sitting back on his heels admiring one. When he spoke about horses he used words like "mighty" and "superior," as if he thought horses were part of God himself.

Mr. Morgan saw us and waved.

"You boys looking for Jimmy?" he asked real nice.

Luther spoke right up. "Yessir. We're figuring on going down fishing. If you can spare him."

"Jim's put in a good day's work already," Mr. Morgan said. He motioned Jim over, then turned to say a gentle word to one of his horses.

Mr. Morgan spoke gentle all the time; like no other man I ever heard. No matter what he had to say, he never raised his voice above this soft windy sound that made you feel like you were real important just because he was taking the time to speak to you.

Jim said his daddy'd likely been born that way. But I believe it was from talking to horses all the time—real coaxing, with that tone when you're wanting an animal to trust you and you've got your hand stretched out, waiting for him to feel safe enough to come close.

Surely, Mr. Morgan was different from most folks. Unfortunately, these days folks who were different made other folks suspicious. That kept Mr. Morgan away from town most always now, sticking close to home—preferring the company of his horses, Jim said.

Jim ran up and the four of us waved good-bye to his dad; then we all walked around to the front of the house, me keeping my eyes on the dirt when we passed by Claire. Her shoes were about all I dared let myself look at, except for a quick glance at that sweet Mary Pickford smile of hers.

We headed past the windbreak and the little fenced area where Jim's dead relations were buried. Then we ran over the footbridge and along the river path to the spot below Suicide Curve—the place on the road where people drive off the edge on a regular basis taking the turn on the hill too fast. A whole team of horses went over one time, and last year Mr. Wattaker wrecked his car so bad it left him crippled for life and as cranky as a nest of hornets.

I only know of one real suicide. Years ago some fellow named Peacock lost his farm to a fire and just didn't have the guts to face life any longer, my daddy said. Threw himself off that place one rainy night. Took three days before they found him floating down there in the river.

We claimed our regular spots high on the sunny rocks a ways up from the bridge, rolled our trousers, and tossed our lines out into the water. Billy griped that he wished his mama would buy him a real fishing pole. He was spoiled, being an only child—had all those toys, always had a pocketful of candy or Wrigley's chewing gum, and got letters from his daddy addressed just to him.

We fished for an hour or so without any bites and with the sun beating down like anything, burning our knees and arms.

"I'm swimming," Billy announced. Stood right there where he was and started to strip off his clothes.

Now, it's not as if there were ever a million people passing by on the bridge, but at least once a day somebody'd go over. And when they did they'd usually wave if they saw us.

Billy didn't care. And as it turned out, after he jumped in and looked cool as could be, paddling around in the ripples, his rump popping above the surface like a buoy, neither did the rest of us. How could we help it?

"Come on in, I dare you!" he shouted, waving his arms and splashing us.

Luther went next. Peeled off everything and hopped right in.

Like always, neither Jim nor I wanted to be last and scrape up against the concept of being called a coward, so we tossed aside our fishing poles, tore off our clothes, and followed the other two into the river, hollering all the time like a couple of banshees.

It was the hollering that did it, I imagine. Sound carries up from water no matter where you are. And the place it carried up to that time was the bridge.

Mrs. Tilley and her granddaughter, Martha, were having themselves an afternoon stroll, walking slowly because of Mrs. Tilley's swollen legs that she probably got from all that delicious rhubarb pie she made . . . walking slowly and admiring the summer scenery.

Whoop-de-do, there we were, splashing around like polliwogs in a puddle, not worrying a whit if our rumps were bobbing on top of the water, or if anyone saw us waggling in the wind when we scrambled up to dive off the rocks.

It was Luther who noticed them first, standing on the bridge, staring down at us like we were some rare species of fish. If you ask me, they were gawking.

"Look there, Granny," I heard Martha say. "Why, isn't that Joey Farrington? And there! I know that's Billy Teale!"

Mrs. Tilley didn't have any trouble recognizing us. Last winter we'd spent time at her house learning to knit—all us boys side by side with the girls, three days a week after school, sitting in a circle knitting socks and mufflers for our soldiers over in Europe.

Now, you might think, so what if she saw us? So what if she knows who we are? What harm can Mrs. Tilley do?

Plenty. Plenty in a big way. Mrs. Tilley was the town's very own gossipy Mata Hari, pretending to be friendly but spying on folks all over the place, always worrying about suspicious goings-on. We knew it wouldn't be long before she'd be cranking up that telephone of hers to ring her friend Mabel Dawes. Mabel had taken over the job of telephone operator since the war broke out. Quick as that, at least ten or twenty of our neighbors would know that four boys had been seen swimming naked by the bridge. And worse, Mrs. Tilley'd be able to name each one of us right down the line.

So there we were, stuck trying to hide our altogether under the water as they stood there pointing at us.

It took Mrs. Tilley way too long to realize she ought to cover her granddaughter's eyes and lead her off that bridge. By the time she thought of it, Jonathan Cass and Winston Brown—two of Harley's friends—had come by to see what they were finding so interesting there in the water. They probably thought it was a crash victim floating down from Suicide Curve, but when those boys saw it was us they laughed out loud and we knew we were in for it. Mrs. Tilley might take care of informing every single adult in town and ruining our reputations by the end of the day, but Jonathan and Winston would round up Luther's brothers in only a matter of minutes.

"Hey there, Johnny," Winston said real loud. "Ain't that little Luther Thornton?"

Beside me, his chin below the water, Billy burbled, "What'll we do?"

"Grab the clothes before Harley and the boys show up!" Jim said.

We paddled fast to the bushes by the bank, scrambling up into the mud and over the rocks to the spot where we'd left our clothes. No telling how bad things would go if Luther's brothers got to them before we did.

"We'd better run," Billy said, gathering his clothes into a muddy mass. "Come on! Let's go!"

I'd just managed to pull my underpants halfway up and was still wiggling them on, when Jim announced in an ominous tone, "There they are."

Sure enough. Like one single fist of meanness, those three big boys were on their way to get us, Harley in the lead, followed by Ray and Arlo.

They were laughing and shouting insults as they came plowing through the brush.

Billy screeched, his voice flying up like a girl's. "Joe! Jim! Hurry!"

None of us bothered to finish dressing. We picked up our clothes, headed out the other side of the thicket, and, just like that army in the headlines, we beat a disordered retreat—out of the bushes, onto the road, and back through town, passing Mr. Lyle and Mr. Peck, the soldier poster, and all those patriotic flags waving howdy—running shoeless and near naked, our fishing poles and our pride long gone behind us.

CHAPTER 5

THAT NIGHT MAMA HARDLY SPOKE to me, having heard first from Mrs. Tilley, then from nearly every other soul in town that my friends and I had been seen running down Main Street in the middle of the afternoon, half naked and covered in mud. She didn't say I'd let her down or shamed the name of Farrington, but I could tell she was feeling it every time she looked at me, her eyes working hard on mine, showing their disapproval as all of us sat down together to write letters to Papa.

Sure enough I wasn't supposed to tell him discouraging things, but I wouldn't have told him about my troubles of the day even if I'd been allowed to. I might have mentioned the swim and getting caught by Mrs. Tilley, but it wouldn't do to say what a fool and coward I'd been, letting Harley and the boys chase me off without my clothes, bringing embarrassment to the whole entire family while he was over in France being so brave and heroic.

I wrote an extra long letter, though—writing, blotting, writing some more, just telling him about the nice weather we'd been having, that the sheep were all doing fine, that I'd been a help around the house.

I figured my staying at the table a long time after the girls were done might give Mama the idea I was making amends. I was hoping she'd believe that her silence and my own shame were punishment enough for what I'd done. But she had other ideas for me.

Next morning she put on her gloves and her hat, then took us uptown to mail our letters and do the shopping. And, of course, to see if a letter had arrived from Papa. She decided we'd walk to the grocery—to conserve gasoline the way the government had told us to, she said. But I knew the real reason Mama wanted me to walk was so I could feel all those eyes looking up to make sure I had on my clothes.

She made me pull Helen in the wagon, and both girls sang all the way into town. Must have sung that new favorite, "Over There," a thousand times.

As we turned the corner onto Main Street, Mama told Alice to take charge of the wagon. Then she straightened her back, motioned that I should take her arm, and paraded me right past Mr. Lyle and Mr. Peck—just to show them and everyone else who might be watching that even though she had an idiot fool for a son, it wasn't going to scare her away from showing her face in town.

They tipped their hats politely. "How do you do, Mrs. Farrington?" said Mr. Peck.

"Fine day, isn't it?" said Mr. Lyle.

"Good morning, gentlemen," Mama said, smiling but not stopping to pass the time of day. I knew they were getting a howl out of seeing me all duded up and shopping with the ladies while they thought back to the state I was in the last time I went by.

After Mama steered me into the hardware store for pushpins and a new clothesline, we walked across the street to the druggist to buy toothpaste and soap, then next door to Jepson's to pick up groceries and the mail. Mama let the girls stay outside, but made me go in to help.

Since Jepson's was both the post office and the grocery store, it had always been the central meeting place in town—especially in winter, when the men would stop by at lunchtime to swap stories around the wood-stove. But that had changed since the war. It was still the post office, but it wasn't the bustling place it used to be, stocked full of canned goods, barrels of flour and sugar, and bins overflowing with fruits and vegetables. Now everybody was Hooverizing—Food Administrator Herbert Hoover's idea of how each and every citizen could help in the war effort. We were conserving food, just like we did gasoline, so there would be more to send to the soldiers. No wheat on Mondays and Wednesdays, no beef on Tuesdays, no pork on Thursdays and Saturdays.

But Jepson's still smelled like ripe apples and coffee. Every time I passed the big bean grinder on the counter by the door, that coffee aroma hit me and I started missing Papa something fierce.

The bell jingled as the door closed behind us and Mr. Jepson popped his head out from the little room at the back to say hello.

When he came out to the counter, Mama handed him our letters.

"And I believe there's a letter for you, Mrs. Farrington," he said, checking the row of post boxes on the wall. He reached up and pulled out our mail.

Mama looked so pleased that for a moment I thought she might just give Mr. Jepson a hug. But of course she didn't. She did what she always did—tucked Papa's letter safely into her pocket without looking at it. She did that every time, and it near drove me crazy. Wasn't she dying to know what Papa had to say?

I knew better than to beg her to open it in public. According to Mama, a letter was a private matter, something to be left for reading when we were at home, alone.

We did our marketing and when we'd finished, Mama took out her little brown shopping book and handed it to Mr. Jepson.

"Five pounds of flour, sixty cents," he said, making a note in Mama's book. "Two cans of soup, twenty-four cents; oats, fifteen cents; three-pound ham, three dollars . . ." He finally finished tallying, then handed the book back to Mama so she could keep track of what she owed.

"Always glad for your business, Mrs. Farrington," he said offering me candy sticks to share with the girls.

I was just putting that candy into my mouth, thinking the day hadn't been so horrible after all, when I heard the doorbell jingle. I turned around, thinking it was probably the girls, but instead, I saw Harley and Ray and Arlo. They swaggered in like they owned the place, all three of them coming my way. I hadn't seen them up close for a month or so. They sure seemed to have grown. Even Arlo had whiskers now.

I felt Harley's eyes on me. I took that fool candy out of my mouth and hid it behind my back. Arlo and Ray grinned, and I half wondered if one of them might decide to come up and give me a shove just for the heck of it, and maybe knock me into the creamed corn display. I stepped close to Mama.

When she looked up and saw them, all three of those boys turned angel, just smiley as could be, tipping their hats.

"Good morning, Mrs. Farrington," they all said at once.

"Hello, boys," Mama said.

Harley knocked Ray in the ribs with his elbow, then stepped forward. "May we carry those outside for you?" he asked. "All those groceries look like they might be a bit too much for Joey here."

Harley held the door open for Mama; then Ray and Arlo carried our boxes out and put them into the wagon.

While Alice and Helen sucked happily on their candy, I just stood there feeling stupid, wishing Luther'd show up to say something sassy to his brothers. That way maybe they'd forget Mama was there and she'd see they were still as rude and mean as ever.

"Have a pleasant day, Mrs. Farrington," Harley said, tipping his cap again as he walked back into the store.

"Now, that was nice of them, wasn't it, Joe?" she said as we headed home. "Seems Harley has done some growing up since his father went away. His mother must be pleased to have the boys home for the summer. I'm sure they're a big help to her."

"Sure," I said. "Bet they do that sort of thing for Mrs. Thornton all the time."

AFTER LUNCH, MAMA STILL wasn't ready to read Papa's letter, so I took off quick as that to meet the fellows over in the Grove. I was pretty sure they'd be there—keeping out of the way of Luther's brothers.

The Pepperwood Grove was the perfect hideout. When we were in first grade we'd discovered it on our own. Or at least we'd thought we had. Papa later showed me his own initials carved into one of the tree trunks.

We kept all kinds of secret stuff hidden there. We had an old *Picture-Play* magazine and a copy of *Sexual Knowledge Illustrated* that Billy'd found in his garage. And we had magazine pictures from the war, clippings of airplanes and warships and no-man's-land—that misty stretch of ground between the German and Allied trenches that folks said was covered with blood and bodies and smoke from artillery fire. All the stuff we hid there was secret, but most of it was probably only important to us. Like the stuff in that box Papa'd talked about, I suppose. Secrets and special things we didn't want to make part of anyone else's business. Billy tried to keep candy there, but bugs got to it. Except for bug invasions, though, the Pepperwood Grove was our territory. It belonged to us, and it was safe.

When I got there, Luther jumped up and asked if I'd come across his brothers. "You see them anywhere, Joe?"

Everyone scowled with worry.

"Just back at Jepson's," I said. "They came butting in to impress my mama. Being grocery-box heroes. She thinks maybe they've grown up some."

"Grown," said Luther, rubbing his arm. "I'll say. We have to shear with them on Friday, you know."

We all moaned.

Billy shook his head. "At least they won't bother us here."

"Speaking of a bother," said Jim, "I've got something here. It's about cooties."

"My daddy says they're itchy as hell," said Luther.

"Yeah," Jim said. "Says here they're a bother near as bad as the Germans."

We sat down on a log and Jim took out a *National Geographic* magazine he'd brought from home. His daddy might not have gone to war but that didn't keep Jim from being interested in it. He kept up on the news same as the rest of us.

"Hey." Billy snatched the magazine out of Jim's hands. "What's this?"

Right there on the page facing that cootie article was

a picture of Billy's hero, Major Billy Bishop, and his plane.

"This is a whole lot more interesting than lice," Billy said, practically poking his nose to the page.

"Yeah," agreed Luther. "Guess nobody's going to win a medal over there just killing bugs."

"Sure enough," I said. "Or taking care of their feet. That's what my daddy likes to tell about. No mention of killing Germans at all."

"Well, Major Billy Bishop's killed plenty," Billy said. "Maybe even got some of those *baby-eating* Germans my mama was telling me about."

We were all listening real close now, and Billy was near frothing at the mouth wanting to tell us.

"She went to the picture show in Maxwell last week. Those Four Minute Men were there. You know, those government men who get up at intermission and tell about what's *really* going on over in Europe?"

All of us nodded. We'd heard a lot of their stories since we got into the war. And every time we heard a new one it was worse than the one before.

"They said Germans were eating Belgian babies. Stole them right out of their cribs and had them for lunch."

"That's ridiculous," Jim said.

"I'm only telling what I was told," said Billy.

"Sounds like a whopper to me," I said.

"That's what they're saying just the same."

"Harley says there are spies all over the place, even here in California," said Luther. "He thinks there are Germans everywhere, ready to shoot us in our sleep."

"I'd shoot them first," Billy said, hopping up to zoom off in his imaginary airplane. "I'd bomb them from the sky."

Luther looked at me and sighed. "While you're at it, maybe you could drop a bomb on my brothers," he said.

We all had a laugh over that.

"I wonder who gets those whoppers going," I said. "Do folks really believe all that stuff? Heck, I wonder if *anyone* knows what's really happening over there."

Luther socked me on the arm. "You sound like your daddy with all that wondering, Joe."

I socked him back, then took out Papa's knife and whittled for a while. "Wonder what it's like to meet a German soldier face-to-face."

"Probably wouldn't have time to think about it much," said Jim. "No time to chat, you know."

"I'd chat with my bayonet," Luther said, poking Jim. "A one-sided conversation."

"Naw." Jim laughed, poking him back. "I'd make my point first."

All three of us started roaring then, pushing each other off that log while Billy zoomed around dropping imaginary bombs.

IT WAS ALMOST BEDTIME when Mama finally opened Papa's letter. After all that war talk in the Grove, I was feeling energized, imagining Papa fixing his bayonet and charging after those Germans. Made me more anxious than ever to know what his letter had to say.

We gathered around her in the living room, Alice clutching her hankie, ready to go teary the minute Mama started to read. Helen was too young to care much one way or the other. She always seemed more interested in fooling around with Mama's shoelaces than in what Papa had to say. Spit went over to the spot by Papa's chair and lay down, her chin on her paws.

" 'My dear loves,' " Mama began.

"They are calling us 'summer soldiers.' In part, I think because we have come so late to the war. But it is mostly due to our missing the terrible winters in the trenches. They say we Americans treat war like a football game. But we have been working hard, marching from sunup to sundown. When we are not marching, we are dodging German snipers. The woods are full of them. . . ."

Helen tugged on Mama's skirt. "What's a sniper, Mama? Is it a bird?"

Mama looked down at Helen. "Maybe," she said gently, brushing her hand over my sister's hair. "Perhaps it is. Now let me read on.

"Here things can change in a flash. In the middle of the darkest night flares light the sky like day. One moment the noise of battle is deafening, the next it is so quiet you can hear the birds singing in the trees nearby."

"See, Mama?" Helen said. "I was right. It was a bird, wasn't it?"

"Mmmm," Mama said, glancing at me. "A bird." She looked back to the letter. "Listen," she said, "Papa wrote us a poem.

"Though stirred from sleep by fiery skies,
Though battles rage athwart the sea,
Warm I am within my heart—
Where you are—near, and here, with me.
        I send you all my love.
                Papa"

We sat quiet for a moment, thinking about Papa, until Mama folded the letter and said it was time to go to bed. "Guess it's the end of another day," she said, that sad look coming up in her eyes.

Spit yawned, then padded into the kitchen. I followed to let her out while Mama took the girls upstairs to bed.

The kitchen was dark, and quiet.

I carried the empty milk bottles out onto the porch, looking into the wide star-filled sky and out across the empty yard, imagining how it would look all lit with flares and artillery fire. Fog was floating up from the ocean and I was sort of enjoying the spooky way it hovered with the chimney smoke just above the river. As I watched it, though, it gave me a chill. It reminded me of something—some misty space I'd seen before, kind of ghostly and all, with the smoke and fog hanging low to the ground.

Shook me when I figured out it was reminding me of that magazine picture we had over in the Grove— the one of no-man's-land way over there in Europe where all the fighting was going on. I'm not sure why it struck me so, but I started feeling lonesome inside, and cold. And, even though I knew I should have been used to it by then, suddenly Papa seemed terribly far away.

CHAPTER 6

Great-aunt Binny telephoned on Wednesday and said she was going to arrive the next afternoon. Mama went into a cleaning frenzy and held all three of us prisoner, putting me to work with the feather duster and carpet sweeper while the girls polished silver and ironed bedsheets.

Then she tied those cushions around me and had me model that dress again. Of course, I made her pull down the shades and swore the girls to secrecy, but they were still getting a big fat kick out of seeing me dressed up like a fancy old begonia.

"Oh, you look so *beau-ti-ful!*" Alice said.

"Curtsey, Joey!" said Helen.

They giggled at me from across the room, over and over, pointing and asking Mama to make me turn and twirl for them. I might have found some humor in the situation, but all the time I was standing there like a fool in that dress, they were doing their own good work over in the corner, sewing red and blue crosses on sashes to wear on the Fourth of July. It made me sick to think my sisters were doing noble deeds that would be making Papa proud while I was standing there worthless as mud wearing Aunt Binny's summer dress and looking like my own private ten-acre garden party.

Helen held up her sash to show me. "Now everyone in town will see that Papa's in the service." I wanted to say they didn't need to make sashes to prove that. Heck, we already had a Red Cross Service Flag hanging in the front window. Everybody in town knew Papa'd gone to war. Just the same as they knew Mr. Morgan hadn't.

When we drove over to Maxwell the next day to pick Binny up at the train station, she was waiting for us on the platform clutching her bumbershoot and pocket-book like she figured someone was about to rob her.

She had come on the train alone, having left Uncle Chester home with a spell of the gout. Mama claimed his stubbornness and ornery attitude gave him that ailment; me, I think Aunt Binny was what brought it on. I figured he was probably looking forward to the time without her. Sure thing, if it was me who had to live with her year-round, I'd be accumulating pains in every portion of my body. Binny was fussy and had peculiar ways. She took Lydia E. Pinkham pills for her nerves and rattlesnake oil to ward off deafness. She sang morning to night, made us wash and change and comb our hair for dinner like we lived a hundred years ago, and she still used a chamber pot at night instead of the indoor toilet.

She saw us pull up at the station and near started weeping, rushing to swallow us in powdery hugs and kisses, wailing all the time about her horrible-horrible-terrifying trip without Uncle Chester along for protection, ninny-fussing about mashers and highwaymen. Oh, yes, it seemed fraidy-cat Aunt Binny was going to be a whole lot of help to Mama.

Right away Binny filled the house with rosy old-lady smells and enough luggage for Pershing's army. I carried her baggage upstairs. Helen and Alice carried her scrapbook. That old thing was about as big as a table and must have weighed fifteen pounds. It was full of stuff she'd collected and things she'd cut from the newspaper—sort of like Papa's box, I imagined. Except she never went anywhere without it and loved to share it with us. Not like Papa, who'd gone and hidden his treasures so well he'd forgotten where they were.

After dinner that night, Alice and I stayed in the kitchen, doing dishes, making ourselves useful so Binny wouldn't think we were such a burden on Mama. I washed and Alice dried. All the time she went on and on about the letter she'd written to Papa.

"I told him I lost a tooth," she said, holding her mouth open for me to see. "And I told him I helped Mama sew curtains."

"And you probably told him lies about me," I said.

"I didn't lie, Joey," she said. "I told him all about how you helped with Mama's sewing. Then I told him how pretty you looked in that dress."

I was about to fling a handful of soapsuds her way when Binny called from the other room for us to gather for a recitation. Binny was wild for oratory and made it clear to all of us that we ought to be too. She thought every kid on earth ought to grow up spouting Charles Kingsley or Henry Wadsworth Longfellow.

"Skill in speaking is as important as having the vote!" Binny said. Every time she came to visit she insisted we learn a new poem. That night she chose a short, easy one, for Helen. By Christina Rossetti. Binny took a spot by the fireplace, put her hand over her heart, and began:

> *"Who has seen the wind?*
> *Neither I nor you:*
> *But when the leaves hang trembling*
> *The wind is passing through. . . ."*

She made us say it over before she recited the next stanza. For Mama's sake, all three of us lined up to practice and made waving motions with our arms to show respect for Binny's enthusiasm—though Papa's quiet style of recitation appealed a whole lot more to me.

After we'd learned it well enough to recite alone, Mama sat down to play the piano and we kids obliged Binny with a round of Authors. Binny won, gathering all the Charles Dickens cards. I'd been trying for Louisa May Alcott, but as it turned out, so had Alice—even though she tricked me into thinking she was saving James Fenimore Cooper by saying more than once how much she liked *The Last of the Mohicans*. Helen liked that book too, as Papa had read it to all of us. But she only went by the faces on the cards and her favorite was Nathaniel Hawthorne. Helen must have played the game a thousand times, but always lost because everyone knew he was the only one she ever tried to collect.

Neither of the girls liked losing, so we turned to other amusements while Mama went on playing for us. Binny shared her scrapbook with the girls and I took up working on a puzzle of *The Signing of the Declaration of Independence* that Papa'd sent to us last Christmas. I'd only gotten as far as Thomas Jefferson's left shoe when the cats started howling outside.

"Joe," Mama said, pausing midmeasure at the piano. "Go out and shoo those mangy cats off, will you? Their squalling's making the hair stand up on my neck."

For some reason, our street had been plagued by cats ever since Papa left. Folks had various theories on it, from blaming Mrs. Higgins down the road for putting fish guts out for them, to old Mr. Appleton's idea that the Germans were at fault somehow.

I took Spit out with me and we crept around the side of the house to sneak up on the cats. I crouched low, wondering if Papa might be somewhere in the dark alone right now, creeping up on the Germans.

Spit sniffed those cats right away, and her fur rose up sharp as a porcupine's. She looked like some kind of crazed phantom there in the moonlight with that weird hairdo and her teeth showing under her lip.

Other cats might have been smart enough to zip off into the darkness before we caught them, but when we got there we only saw one. One was enough. It was a big yowly tiger cat, puffed up and about as angry as a cat can get and still stay inside its skin.

Well, the cat saw Spit, and Spit saw the cat, and there we go one-two-three, natural-born enemies ready to spill blood right there in the yard in front of me. It promised to be real exciting.

But nothing happened. That old tom, all snarly and fat, with his back arched like a bow, just stood his ground there in the corner by the fence, growling and hissing like nothing I'd ever seen before.

Spit had quite surely never met a cat that wasn't afraid of her and she plain had no idea what to do about it. She whined and took a step forward, but that cat didn't run, he just got madder and madder.

"Go get it, Spit," I said, ready to find a chunk of wood and heave it at the old feline if he didn't get going on his own pretty soon.

Spit didn't budge. I turned around, about to holler at her, when an eerie, bloodcurdling yowl came rising up behind me.

Fast as that, I scrambled up the steps, across the porch, and through the door.

Spit beat me into the kitchen.

Alice was waiting there, grinning at us.

"Fraidy-cats?" she said.

She spun around and went dancing back into the living room, leaving me standing there feeling as foolish as I had when I was wearing that dumb old flowered dress of Binny's.

Spit came slinking up beside me.

"Coward," I said, pushing her aside. "You're even more worthless than me."

CHAPTER 7

IN THE MORNING when I got up and let Spit out, she ran into the yard wagging her tail like last night never happened.

Sure thing, it was peaceful out; sheep bawling away on the hills; the wet grass taking on a sparkle in the sun. For the life of me I couldn't figure why I'd been so spooked by that tomcat. It wasn't as if I'd been frightened by any German spies trying to creep up on me, or even by the Thornton boys. How much of a coward was I, to be scared of a dumb old cat?

I was thinking on this when Mama called me in.

"You nearly done chopping that kindling, Joe? Harley rang up. He's expecting you at seven. He wants to start shearing by eight."

Just hearing the name Harley, I could feel a stomachache coming on. I'd forgotten all about shearing. Today was the day. And we'd be working with Luther's brothers again. This time, without Mr. Morgan.

I, for one, wasn't looking forward to it in the least. I

set down the hatchet, picked up an armful of wood, and headed for the house.

Mr. Morgan had offered to help shear, but Harley still wouldn't have anything to do with him. He was obliged to include Morgan's sheep, though, since the Morgans had already put up the money for two extra shearing men to come over from Maxwell.

I dumped the kindling in the bin on the back stoop, hung my jacket by the icebox, then went inside. Binny and Mama and the girls were already sitting at the table, eating mush.

I freshened the fire, then went over and sat down with them, hurrying through my breakfast, washing my cornmeal mush down with a quick glass of milk.

Helen grinned at me from across the table. She was wearing a silly green cap left over from last winter that she'd made part of her daily costume. Mama snatched it off her head. "No hats at the table, young lady," she said, then looked at Alice and added, "No books either."

I guess since Binny was there, Mama figured she needed to reform our manners.

Alice wasn't paying attention. She was too busy reading, her spoon straight up in one hand, a twirl of her hair in the other, *The Secret Garden* open where her bowl should have been.

Helen stared down at her mush and poked it with her spoon.

"Lumps," she said.

"There's always lumps," mumbled Alice, still reading.

"Lumps make me choke," Helen said.

I was about to suggest she give her mush to the dog if she was so particular, when Binny touched her hand. "Dear," Binny said, straightening herself. "To argue and complain over such frivolous matters makes me worry you have forgotten the hardship the rest of the world is suffering during these difficult times."

Mama looked at me. From her expression I could tell she was wishing it was Papa instead of me sitting across the table from her.

"Alice," Binny said, "would you be so kind as to put that book aside and offer your sister one reason why she ought to be grateful for mush, regardless of lumps?"

"Because the children are starving in Belgium," Alice said dutifully without looking up.

Binny nodded sternly and turned back to Helen. "Thank you, Alice. Now, Helen, a reason from you, please."

Helen squirmed in her chair. It crossed my mind that she might be too young to come up with an answer. She'd had a birthday last month, but still, how much could a six-year-old know or understand about the war?

Alice closed her book, looked at Helen, then leaned to whisper into her ear.

Helen made a face. "Because soldiers don't have anything to eat but bully and cold fat."

Binny scowled. "I believe that's bully *beef* and cold fat *bacon*, Helen," she said.

Mama smiled patiently. "Not nearly as nice as hot cornmeal mush, now, is it? Even with lumps."

"Even with lumps," Helen agreed, making that face again. "But may I send my mush to Papa just the same? I bet he's awful hungry if that's all he has to eat."

That lumpy mush turned over in my belly. Might have been the idea of pickled beef and cold bacon doing it, but I was reasonably sure it was the thought of having to spend the day working for Harley and the boys. And knowing that Mr. Morgan wouldn't be there to keep the peace.

"Best get on now, Joe," Mama said. "Harley will be waiting."

Helen might have been able to muster enough courage to swallow those lumps, but it wasn't anything like the courage *I* was going to have to call up. Going off to work for Luther's brothers felt like heading into battle.

OF ALL THE THORNTON BOYS, Harley was the only one who could do any sort of shearing at all. While Ray and Arlo probably couldn't cut a straight row of grass, much less clip the fleece off a kicking sheep, Harley was good at it, and got paid to shear for other folks in the valley. But ours was a job that needed more than one set of shears. So they'd hired on another fellow named Rollins and his partner, Karl Bauer, to come out and help.

As it turned out, though, Rollins showed up alone.

"Bauer's left these parts," he said, spitting tobacco

juice onto the floor of the shed. "Left a time back, in spring. His name, you know. And the accent. Folks asked questions. Can't be helped. It's the times, I suppose." He spat again and rolled up his sleeves. "You boys ready to work?"

So Mr. Bauer'd moved out of Maxwell because he was German. Just as well, I figured, since Luther's brothers had so much to say about foreigners these days. Lots of people did, in fact. Hadn't Mrs. Tilley dug up her garden and pulled out all her bachelor's buttons when she found out they were Germany's national flower? And hadn't we done without Great-aunt Binny's pfeffernuss last Christmas because nobody was making German cookies? Heck, I'd even heard some fellow named Praeger actually got himself lynched in St. Louis, just because he was born in Germany.

Even though Bauer was gone, Rollins was up to the job. He was skinny, but he was all muscle, and he could grab a cranky ewe between his knees and have her clipped quicker than anything. Harley wasn't near as fast, but he was earnest. He'd be working and shouting and cussing along with Rollins all day while Ray and Arlo did the grabbing and hobbling. Arlo was especially efficient at kicking difficult sheep in the nose so they'd get knocked stupid long enough for him to throw them down.

"At least you idiots have your pants on today," he said when we arrived.

Ray laughed. Then he shouted at us to get to work. "And I don't want to hear a peep out of any of you squirts. Kids your age in the cities are working twelve-hour days, seven days a week!"

Ray was about the biggest bully walking on two feet. He always shouted orders out of the side of his mouth like he was boss man on a chain gang, and I knew he wouldn't let any of us stop for a swig of water or a pee. Heck, we'd probably sweat so hard the wool would get wet.

He divided us into twos: two outside, shooing sheep into the shed; two inside, gathering, folding, and tying the wool.

To start, it was Jim and me on gathering and tying, which immediately proved unfortunate.

"You, Jim, how's your daddy?" Ray asked right off.

Of course this question didn't require an answer. We all knew it wasn't a pleasantry. So Jim didn't answer with more than a soft, halfhearted "Fine."

Not enough for Ray. Not enough for Arlo either. "Ray here asked you how your daddy is, Jimmy. Didn't you hear him?"

"My daddy's fine," Jim said.

"I *bet* he's fine," said Ray. "Finer than any other daddy around. He's sure not over there fighting the war. He's not over there getting blinded and burned by poison gas."

All morning, Jim and I stayed there listening to those boys chew on Mr. Morgan. All that time, Jim kept quiet, controlling himself and not letting it get to him—sort of like his daddy would have handled it, I suppose.

The only feature of the morning worth remembering was when Claire came by with a basket of chicken sandwiches for us. Best I ever ate in my life.

But then, after lunch, it was Luther's turn to work inside.

Ray wasn't ready to quit tormenting Jim. "You got some of that Hun blood in you, Jimmy?" he asked. "Is that why your daddy stayed home?"

Arlo kicked a shorn fleece in Jim's direction. "Naw," he said. "That whole Morgan family's only got yellow blood running in their veins."

I was on my way out to help Billy in the corral, but I stuck around inside the shearing shed when I saw Luther's face start to pucker and go crimson. He'd always had a bad tongue ready to spit fire at anyone who annoyed him, but you'd think growing up in the same house as Harley and Ray and Arlo, he would have known better than to backtalk any of them. But Luther wasn't ever smart that way.

He hooked his thumbs in his belt loops, puffed out his chest, and stepped up to Arlo.

"Take it back, Big Mouth!" he said, shoving his chin out as far as it would go, just as if he was daring Arlo to take a swing at it. And sure enough, Arlo did. Landed Luther flat on his rump in a pile of sheep poop.

"You rotten sassy little runt!" Arlo yelled, picking poor Luther up by the collar. "Want to tell me to shut up again?"

Like I said, Luther was a slow learner. "I said take it

back, Big Mouth!" he sputtered. His bottom lip was bleeding pretty good by now.

Arlo held Luther there, then pulled his hair back real hard, ready to have at him again. And it looked like Ray was about ready to have a go too, when Harley got tired of them wasting time, dropped the ewe he was working on, and kicked Arlo in the knee. Guess he'd learned that from Mr. Thornton.

Arlo screeched, dropped Luther, and bent over to grab his leg.

Luther didn't take a second to think about his next move. He went right behind Arlo, hauled off, and put his boot into his backside.

Ray got a hand on Luther then. And Arlo muscled back in, while Jim and I just stood there gaping. Old Rollins didn't pay any mind to it. He kept on clipping away. I guess because he was getting good money for the job he was doing.

The brawl went on another moment or so, till Harley decided everybody ought to get back to work. "Quit!" he shouted, adding a couple of cuss words to the order. "He's mine!"

Harley picked up his shears, took two steps over to his brothers, and yanked Luther away from them. "You need a good lesson, Baby Boy," he said, grinning about as wide as the Panama Canal and putting Luther between his knees. Luther made a good fight of it, more than any old sheep ever did, kicking and hollering and trying to bite the inside of Harley's leg. But Harley held him, and sheared his head as bald as the backside of a freshly mowed ewe.

Luther wriggled free, stood up, and spat the blood out of his mouth. "You're nothing but Hun crap!" he said to Harley. "And you others too!" he shouted at Ray and Arlo.

Jim looked at me. I glanced through the door at Billy. He was already halfway across the corral, heading for the far fence. I looked back at Jim.

Then I grabbed one of Luther's arms and Jim grabbed the other, and we hauled him out of that shearing shed like it was about to burst into flames.

It was clear the war had begun. And it was equally clear to us, as we hightailed it out of there like a pack of cowards, that so far, we were losing.

CHAPTER 8

WE ALL MADE UP EXCUSES as to why we'd left before the shearing was done, but as it turned out, nobody's was good enough.

Early the next morning Luther's mother rang Mama to report on Harley's version of the facts.

"I hear Luther got a haircut yesterday," Mama said when she hung up the receiver.

"Harley did it," I said.

"Mrs. Thornton has given Luther extra chores as punishment for running out on the job," Mama said. "She suggested that I do the same for you."

Even without explaining the situation to her, I knew Mama would be fair. She was much more inclined than Mrs. Thornton to take note of the possibility that part of the blame might have rested on Luther's brothers. But she said she didn't want Mrs. Thornton to think she'd taken her suggestion with disregard.

"It might be best if you stayed home and played with Alice and Helen today, Joe. At least until Luther is free from his tasks," Mama said. "It will please the girls. They've so wanted to spend time with you."

The whole concept took me by surprise.

Last summer, as I remember, my sisters had spent their playtime quietly tucked away somewhere pretending to be fairy princesses and dressing up their dolls. It was a whole lot of ribbons and silliness so it wasn't too often that they'd pester me to play.

Recently, though, I'd noticed they'd been sort of wild and strange. It took me a time to figure it out, but it seems they were playacting the roles of those serials "The Perils of Pauline" and "The Hazards of Helen." I haven't the foggiest notion where they picked up that inspiration, but there they were, pretending they were about to die, giving in to fits of wailing for help and leaping over furniture.

After breakfast Helen stepped right into the part of her namesake, and Alice didn't waste any time insisting we call her Pauline. They dressed me in an old curtain and a lampshade hat and named *me* Jailbreak Joe. "You're the villain," Alice explained, tying the curtain around my neck with a length of twine. "You capture us and we get away is all. It's easy."

"You have to tie us up to the train tracks," said Helen, "and lock us in the smokehouse, then light it on fire, then drive us to the edge of the cliff . . ."

Well, Spit moved out and took up residence under the house, and by lunchtime I was wishing most heartily that I could trade places with Papa.

But the situation got worse after lunch. Alice's friend Laura Butterworth came over. I made an earnest protest, but Mama insisted I be polite. Hard to understand how part of being polite was to put on my most dastardly expression and run around spouting things like "Die, damsel! Die!" while I tied all the girls to the kitchen chairs and locked them in the closet.

Must say, though, it did give me some satisfaction. But when I saw Luther and Billy and Jim coming through the back door, I dropped the curtain and tried to regain some composure by swaggering in my most manly fashion.

"Hey there, fellas!" I said calmly.

Helen waved when she saw them. "Hey there, Luther!"

"Hiya," he said back, stepping around her like she was a poison mushroom. "Nice cap."

"Nice haircut," Helen sassed back.

"Do you want to play too?" asked Laura, smiling at the boys.

Jim was polite and shook his head.

Luther stuck me in the side with his elbow. "Let's get out of here."

Just then Billy stepped forward like he was ready to take the girls up on the invitation. He reached into his pocket, pulled out a roll of Pep-O-Mint Life Savers, and offered one to Laura.

"Didn't your brother Frank join up?" he asked.

"He's in Italy," she said, popping the candy into her mouth. "They made him a flyer. He drops bombs."

"Wow," Billy said, his eyes starting to sparkle. Jim shot me a look. Both of us could see trouble coming.

"Better go," I said, shoving Billy toward the door.

"We've got business. Important business." It wouldn't do to have him start into his flying routine right here in front of the girls.

Luther's mouth took care of it. "Done talking to the ladies, Billy?" he said. "Or are you planning on staying for tea?"

Two seconds. Only two. Then Billy was after us, across the kitchen and out the door, cursing wildly, his face as purple as a plum.

It was hot enough for swimming, but we knew the Grove was the only place we wouldn't happen upon the Thornton boys.

The minute we got there, Jim and Billy started carrying on like they'd lost their minds. Jim had just read *Tarzan of the Apes* and took to whooping and hollering and swinging from the trees while Billy went zooming around as usual. Luther remarked that we should have left both of them to play with the girls.

He and I took out our stash of magazines and settled in to read for a while. I read about Thomas Edison, and artichoke farms, and that revolution over in Russia. Then about an archeological expedition where some fellows were looking for Troy but all they dug up was a lot of dumb junk. Hairpins and buttons and broken pots. Sounded something like what Papa said he'd buried in that old box of his. I wondered what people would think a thousand years from now if they dug that box up. Probably not much. Made me wonder just then why Papa thought it was so dang important that it should take up all our time together that last night before he went away.

Between artichokes and hairpins and thinking about Papa's box, my mind was wore out, so I lay back in the cool leaves and looked up at the sky. High feathery clouds were floating by up there above the trees. It got me so drifty and faraway in the head that before I knew it I was wondering if it was windy across the ocean in Europe. And I was wondering about Papa. Where was he? Was he okay?

I rolled over and kicked Luther in the side. "Hey, Luther," I said. "What do you hear from your daddy? What's he writing home about these days?"

"Same as last time," he said. "That he's over there in France blowing up the Germans. What about yours?"

Luther looked eager as anything for me to give him some news.

"The same," I said, just like there was nothing unusual about it. "Blowing up Germans."

Queer how things had changed. Papa used to write about his feet; now he was writing about snipers in the trees. Used to be "I Didn't Raise My Boy to Be a Soldier"; now even my little sisters were singing "Over There." We had beefless Tuesdays, no summer Olympics, and now when I read the paper I checked the casualty reports before the comics.

And here we were, talking about the war like it was a Saturday baseball game.

That thought made a strange feeling come up inside me. Either that, or it was all the racket kicking up across the Grove. Jim had started making ape sounds to accompany Billy's zooming. It was turning into a regular circus over there.

Suddenly Billy buzzed our way, zoomed in beside me and Luther, and said, "Smells like smoke."

Well, smoke on a hot June afternoon is like a full-out alarm, so none of us dallied. We climbed the hill, checked in the gulch shrubbery, scanned the valley—no smoke.

"I don't smell it up here," Billy said. "It's down there, and I'm pretty sure it's not regular smoke. Pretty sure it's cigars."

We knew about cigars. We'd all tried them last fall, all turned green and woozy. Laying on our backs in the Grove smoking away, we felt smart as all get-out. Till we stood up, that is. Luther actually lost his lunch in the ditch on the way home.

Still, we knew where we'd gotten those smokes—Luther's brother Ray. "They've been here," Luther said, poking around the log where we usually sat. Sure enough, mixed in with the moss and leaves and hidden salamanders and slugs was a small pile of cigar butts. "Look like dog turds," Jim remarked.

We stayed real still then, watching the trees and the hillside for a sign of Harley and the other boys.

"Do you suppose they're hiding?" Billy asked, taking a step closer to the rest of us. We were huddled together like kittens, practically mewling too.

I was hoping real hard Luther wouldn't answer, sure if he did something would come from his mouth that'd get us into deep hot water if his brothers were out there listening.

Luther peered up into the trees, nosing the wind like an old hound dog sniffing trouble. "They're out there somewhere," he said. "I can smell the stink of 'em."

I believe if I had brothers, I'd feel a whole lot different about them than Luther felt about his. I used to think he had an orneriness toward them because of the way they knocked him around. But sometimes I get the idea that if he'd just keep his trap shut, maybe they'd be a whole lot nicer to him.

"Let's go," I said, holding my breath and hoping Luther wasn't feeling the urge to get his lip bloodied again.

"Not yet," he said. "We've got to make a stand."

"Aw, come on," Billy said. "It ain't worth it right now. You already got us into enough trouble with Harley yesterday."

Then there they were, all three of them, standing ahead of us on the path like a pack of hungry wolves and pelting us with dirt clods.

"I'll get the chubby redhead," Arlo said, zeroing in on Billy. Then he spied me. "I'll get that Joey Farrington too."

"I've got dibs on that yellow-blooded Morgan kid," said Ray.

Harley had his sights on Luther, coming at him all barrel-chested and fuming. "I've got the bald one," he said.

Well, turned out none of us, not even Luther, was willing to take them on.

"We're just leaving," Billy piped in, ducking away from a flying clod. "Just leaving right this minute."

"Yeah," I said, pulling Luther by the arm. "Just leaving."

Harley got a big kick out of it and started laughing. "Make sure you girls don't come back," he said.

Ray was still hot on spilling some of that yellow blood he kept claiming ran in Jim's veins, but we were already on our way. Billy'd made it out to the road by the time we caught up with him. The four of us ran all the way to town without looking back even once to see if Harley and the others were following.

We split up and headed home after that, none of us wanting to talk about what had happened. We all felt too lousy. Miserable, as a matter of fact. We'd lost the Grove, and we hadn't even been brave enough to put up a fight.

CHAPTER 9

OUR SPIRITS WERE MIGHTY run down and sunk after that defeat, and we were all pretty much feeling sorry for ourselves—especially when Luther told us his brothers had gotten their hands on all the stuff we'd hidden in the Grove. But I couldn't look to Mama for consolation. She was too busy getting ready for the Fourth of July, storing up sausages and pies and planning out what the girls were going to wear. And she'd turned frantic with Binny's stay—washing and ironing and sweeping and weeding, and all the time listening to Binny sing. She looked sore in need of peace and relaxation.

Binny must have noticed, though I'm not so sure her remedy was too helpful to Mama. The day before the Fourth, I came in for lunch to find Mama dressed in a Chinese robe Binny'd brought from the city and sipping some kind of strange-smelling tea. Across the room, Binny was at the stove, showing off to the girls how she could flip a pancake as good as that actor Fatty Arbuckle.

I decided to visit the dog and go out and pick a few peas.

That's what I was doing, when Binny's big old singing voice came sailing over the yard. " 'Oh my dar-ling, oh my dar-ling, oh my darling Clem-en-tine . . .' " she wailed away, croaking up and down the scale like a frog with laryngitis. Spit was looking puzzled, probably trying to figure what sort of critter she was aiming to attract, when Luther came running up to the house, waving his arms and pale as milk, crying, "What is it? What is it?"

"It's just Great-aunt Binny," I told him.

"What's she doing? Having a baby?"

"Naw, she's just singing."

" '. . . lost and gone for-ev-er. Dread-ful sor-ry, Clem-en-tine!' "

"Sounds like a love song," Luther said real thoughtful.

"Yeah," I said. "I think she's singing to Uncle Chester. He's home in San Francisco so I guess she's got to sing real loud."

I gave Luther a handful of peas.

"Harley and them have a whole sack of rotten vegetables hid out in the barn," he said.

"Why's that?"

"They're saving up for tomorrow. Think they're planning to go after anybody who's not looking patriotic. Anybody who doesn't sing 'The Star Spangled

Banner' loud enough. Like that. Hey, Billy said every-body's up to the picnic grounds digging the roasting pit. You want to go? Want to watch them do the dig-ging?"

I was game for near about anything to escape Aunt Binny's operetta—even taking a chance on coming across Luther's brothers. So I said yes, though digging wasn't my favorite thing to watch. I took some peas to the kitchen, then ran off with Luther. We met Billy and Jim on the way.

THE FOURTH OF JULY was always about as big a deal as anything in our valley. And this year, with so many of our men and boys off fighting in the war, it was a hundred times more of a big deal than usual.

All the way through the middle of town, folks were hanging from ladders and streetlamps, stringing up banners and flags. Everyone was decorating to show their loyalty. Mr. Motherby, the retired music teacher from the high school over in Maxwell, had come out to practice with the shopkeeper band in the field over be-hind Jepson's. As we passed by, they set to with the music, sending drum booms and piccolo tweets up and down Main Street.

Unfortunately, when we got to the picnic grounds, Harley and the boys were there.

"Hey! The Hobby Horse Gang!" Arlo shouted when he saw us.

He and Ray left the digging and sidled up to Jim.

Ray leaned close, to whisper in Jim's ear. "Want to try your hand with a shovel, Jimmy? Dig a few trenches since your daddy won't?"

Arlo laughed. "We all know Jimmy's too puny to pack a shovel!"

"Thought maybe we could roast a Morgan instead of a pig this year," said Ray. "What do you think, boys? Sound tasty?"

About then Mr. Hicks, the apparent foreman of the project, started making eyes like he was going to put us kids to work if we didn't quit distracting his digging crew, so we took off for the river.

We were walking along the path talking this and that about Mrs. Tilley's rhubarb pie and fireworks and staying up late, when Billy had a sudden fit of aerial inspiration and sped off zooming with his arms spread out. Must have taken Jim's train of thought along with him, because right out of the blue, Jim said, "Don't look like it'll be too much fun this year."

I thought this was a pretty strange thing to say, seeing as how the rest of us had just been discussing what a great time we were going to have setting off explosions and eating all that barbecue. It was one night in the year we were actually going to be allowed to run around wild without grown-ups worrying us to death.

I got it then, slow-witted fellow that I am. It was about his daddy.

"You're going, aren't you?" I asked.

Billy flew in and took hold of Jim's arm. "You have to go," he said. "It's tradition."

"I didn't say I wasn't going," said Jim, pulling away from Billy. "I just said it wouldn't be much fun."

"Hey, Jim. Why'd you say that?" Luther asked.

"Just because."

"Well, just because why?"

I had to kick Luther. He could be so dim sometimes. He looked ready to belt me, but then I think he got it too.

"Yeah," he said, picking up a rock and tossing it across the road at an old apple tree. "Probably won't. My mama's bringing sixteen hundred of our relatives along this year. Including cousin Betty Jane."

We all knew Betty Jane had a serious all-out crush on Luther and had a tendency to want to try to kiss him whenever she visited.

"Yeah," said Billy, catching on at last. "We've got so much family coming in, I'm probably going to have to sleep in the woodshed. It won't be fun at all."

I wondered if Jim was right. I wondered who I'd run the three-legged race with now that Papa wasn't going to be there. And what about the baseball game? Things were sure going to be a lot different without Papa playing third base like he did every year. Come to think of it, the best half of the team was gone off to France or some other faraway place. Maybe there wouldn't even be a baseball game. Or a three-legged race. Now *that* was about as unpatriotic as you could get, as far as I was concerned.

• • •

WHEN I GOT HOME that afternoon, Binny was still running up and down the scales. One look at Mama and I knew my aunt's prescription hadn't helped a bit. She looked positively haggard. When she asked me to take the girls out to the pump to wash their hair, I had to agree. I went into the living room to fetch Helen away from her paper dolls.

She saw me and pulled that cap of hers down hard. "I don't want *you* to do it!" she squealed. "You'll pull my hair and get soap in my eyes!" She crossed her arms over her chest and stuck out her chin like a bulldog.

I didn't waste time reasoning with her. This was one battle I was going to win. I swooped over, lifted her up, slung her over my shoulder, and headed for the door. Paid no mind at all to her wailing at me.

I stumbled out onto the porch and headed down the path toward the pump, with Helen thumping my back with her fists like she was practicing drums for Mr. Motherby's band.

"You've got her upside down," Alice said calmly from the porch.

"Let me go!" Helen wailed.

"You've got her upside down," Alice said again. She skipped down the steps and caught up to me.

"Joey," she said, tugging on my sleeve. "You've got her upside down. You're going to be sorry."

"Sorry?" I snapped at her. "No, *you'll* be sorry, Alice. You give me trouble and I'll have *you* upside down too!"

I surprised myself. It sounded an awful lot like Harley Thornton's voice was coming out of me.

It didn't bother Alice. She just grinned and stepped away from me.

Well, that's about the time Helen shrieked so loud it sounded like I was cutting her head off. Then all of a sudden she went sort of limp on my shoulder, let out a little moan, and threw up all down the back of my trousers.

Fastest I ever dropped anything in my whole life.

I thought Alice was going to split open laughing.

Helen's lip was starting to quiver like she was going to pitch into a fit of bawling or throw up again, but she didn't. She took one look at the back of my pants and went into hysterics right along with Alice, both of them howling as they made their way to the pump.

"Ah, now!" Alice said, grinning over at me as she filled the bucket. "Looks like Jailbreak Joe needs a washing."

"Yes, he does!" Helen agreed. "He needs a lot more than a shampoo!"

Alice had a naughty look in her eye. "Let's give it to him," she said.

Then whoop-de-do, there they came. Pauline and Helen as the bucket brigade, chasing after me.

If I'd smelled better I might have fought harder to get away. I let them catch me before I reached the porch. All that cold water felt good. But I didn't let on to the girls. I chased them back to the pump, took up the bucket myself, and gave them a douse.

Pretty soon we were all soaked. All shampooed and lathered. All standing there in the yard stripped down to nearly nothing, me laughing like I was a little kid again.

Binny must have quit singing long enough so she and Mama could finally hear the commotion. Both of them came running outside waving wooden spoons.

Binny stopped on the porch, spoon aloft, shaking her head and muttering about wild animals before she went back inside.

Mama went inside too, then came out with an armload of towels.

She brought them to us and sat down by the pump while she rubbed Helen's hair.

Around us, twilight was dimming down the far reaches of the yard. A cool breeze came in little puffs up from the river. Everything was taking on a peaceful softness—the trees and bushes, the porch, the house.

"Look," Alice said, pointing to the sky.

We all looked up.

"It's the moon," Helen said, her face poking out from behind the towel. " 'I see the moon and the moon sees me,' " she recited. " 'God bless the moon and God bless me.' "

It was a fat yellow moon, just starting up into the sky over the trees at the top of the valley.

Beside me, Mama reached up and repinned the back of her hair. "Shall we stay outside to watch it rise?" she asked, her face softening in the light.

"Until it's dark?" asked Alice.

"If you'd like," Mama said. "Dinner can wait. And so can Binny, for that matter." She smiled and hugged us close in a bundle. I leaned against her, feeling safe like I used to when I was small.

CHAPTER 10

IN THE MORNING, THE GIRLS got all done up in matching bows and stockings, and Mama put on her pearls and the big blue hat with the white flowers that Papa liked the best. She made me wash and put on clean trousers, and worse, made me wear a tie. She insisted I be presentable for the picture she planned to have us sit for after the picnic.

When everyone was ready to go, Mama helped the girls put on their sashes, then came over to straighten my tie. "So handsome," she said, kissing my cheek. She tucked a clean handkerchief into my shirt pocket. One of Papa's. It had his monogram on it. "Please be a gentleman today, Joe. Make me and your papa proud."

I thought about Papa as we walked to town to meet the parade. I wondered what he was doing. Wondered if he was watching a parade. According to the newspapers, everyone in France was celebrating the Fourth of July this year. I wondered if it was already over where he was, so far away.

Our parade was set to start like always at eleven o'clock, so by ten-thirty we had our place staked out on the sidewalk to watch it go by.

Every single local veteran—from two of Teddy Roosevelt's Rough Riders to a couple of Civil War soldiers who looked old enough to have fought in the Revolution—appeared in full dress uniform, showing off medals and waving flags. The Red Cross ladies marched down the middle of the street carrying an enormous banner that flipped and flopped so hard in the wind it nearly knocked over Billy's mother as she tried to hold up one end. And the Temperance League was not to be left out, making sure we all saw how strongly their members felt about the sins of alcohol. Binny was all for the temperance cause, seeing as how Uncle Chester's imbibing made him howl with the gout. And, of course, both she and Mama cheered when the suffrage women went by.

I stood on my toes to see if I could find any of the other fellows. Billy was across the street on the sidelines, watching his mama go by with that banner. Luther, looking mighty miserable, was down a bit, on the corner, standing between his mama and his cousin Betty Jane. Harley and the other boys were there too. Ray had hold of a suspicious-looking burlap sack, and even from where I was I could see an ambush in his eyes.

I didn't catch sight of Jim until a minute later, and it was his daddy I noticed first. Mr. Morgan looked nice, dressed up in a white shirt and wearing a new hat. He and the rest of the family were standing back against the grove of trees on the little rise by the baseball field, apart from the rest of the crowd.

Mr. Motherby struck up "The Star Spangled Banner" and the men took off their hats. The band of shopkeepers had done a nice job practicing all that time. They outdid themselves on a rendition of that patriotic song that actually stayed on key.

Aunt Binny was standing beside me waving a little flag. She couldn't help herself and broke into full song, taking the high notes all the way to Mars.

After the parade passed, we were treated to a long, rambling speech from Mr. Carter, the president over at Valley Bank. "We here at home must be soldiers too!" he shouted. "We must act like our brave troops overseas. We at home must be patriots; we must be heroes; we must make sacrifices!"

The crowd roared.

Then Mr. Appleton, who'd fought in General Grant's army, hobbled onto the stage and encouraged all of us to make sure to help pay for the war by filling our Liberty Bond books with stamps.

"Lick a stamp and lick the Kaiser," he shouted, almost as loud as Mr. Carter had. "Lick a stamp!" he yelled again.

Then we yelled back, "Lick the Kaiser!"

"Lick a stamp!"

"Lick the Kaiser!"

Flags were waving, banners were flapping, Binny was fanning herself like she was planning on flying off with the rocket's red glare. Took everybody at least five minutes to cool down and catch their breath.

In that time I looked back to where I'd seen Jim. Mr. Morgan was standing all alone now, by the trees, his hat in his hand.

I think I was the only one watching when that rotten old tomato came whizzing through the air and hit him square in the middle of his chest. For a moment he just stood there, staring down at the wet orange circle it left on his shirt. Then, without even looking up, he wiped his hand over the spot, turned around, and walked off in the direction of home.

I don't believe anyone else witnessed that sorry scene, except for those big Thornton boys, of course. I looked around for Jim and Claire, and was glad when I couldn't find them.

Nobody else had a chance to notice, because Mr. Motherby struck up the band with "Yankee Doodle," and pretty soon everyone was singing away and pretending to stick feathers in their caps.

When the music died down, Mrs. Tilley gathered herself together and read the salute of praise she'd written to that young poet Joyce Kilmer, who was fighting over in France. Aunt Binny wept like a baby, and by the end of it I was so ready to get going with some action, I probably would have agreed to let Betty Jane be my partner for the three-legged race.

But then Reverend Belden took the stage and a real solemnness came over the crowd as he began reading the names of the men from our neck of the woods who had died or gone missing overseas. He started with Andrew Marble, sending old Mrs. Marble into a fit of crying. The list wasn't long, thank goodness, but then he read off the names of all the other servicemen who'd joined up or been drafted. When he read Papa's name, Mama gripped my shoulder, then reached into my pocket for Papa's handkerchief. I could hear her behind me, sniffing softly. She was holding us all so close I nearly started bawling myself.

ALL THAT SPEECHIFYING and reading off of names was tolerable, I suppose, when you thought about how many members of the town baseball team we were going to have to do without this year. It seemed only fitting to include them somehow in the day's celebration. And I guess the folks on the organizational committees and all those aging vets from past wars figured it was only honorable to have such a dramatic show of patriotism.

But as the day went on and we all headed into having a good time and eating too much barbecue, it turned out the easiest way to show dedication and devotion and be patriotic was to talk bad about folks like Karl Bauer and George Morgan.

I could feel it like electricity, a prickly sensation in the air that made you walk a ways around certain people because they had their eyes hooked on you kind of funny.

Like when the fellows and I went by the Fultons' picnic table and the folks there all of a sudden went sort of still and quit talking, almost like they were waiting to decide which of them was going to make the first insulting remark.

In that case it was Catherine Fulton's uncle Larry, who set down the pickle he was gnawing on and pointed straight at Jim.

"It's that slacker Morgan's kid, isn't it?" he said, not so much as a question but more to call the fact to everyone's attention. You'd never know by his talk that he'd been one of Papa's friends, and Mr. Morgan's too, before the war. Someone said he'd tried to join up along with Papa and the others but the army didn't take him because he had flat feet.

Jim picked up his pace.

Luther slowed down, and for a moment I worried he'd forgotten that Uncle Larry weighed about three hundred pounds without his boots on, and that Luther's head probably didn't come any higher than his belt buckle.

"Where's your daddy today?" Uncle Larry hollered out at Jim.

I gave Luther a shove and he kept walking.

It didn't get any better. Everywhere we went folks hushed up and pointed at Jim. And some said lots worse to him than Catherine's uncle. Some said things so mean I know they'd have made me cry if they were about Papa. It hurt bad for nobody to remember what a nice man George Morgan was. What did it matter if he didn't want to be a war hero? What difference did it make?

Like always, it made a big difference to Luther's brothers, especially Ray, who was wearing three flags stuck into his cap and a badge with a big old eagle on it.

They caught up to us at the three-legged race.

"I'm not racing," Jim said.

"How come?" I asked.

"No partner," he said.

I pointed out that I didn't have one either. "You can race with me," I said. "We could whip everybody good, the two of us. We're quicker by a mile than Luther and Billy."

"Don't particularly want to race this year," he said. But I knew he must want to. After all, he and Mr. Morgan took second place last year.

"Well, *I* do," I said. "And I need a partner, so come on."

I probably ought to have listened to what was on his mind behind his words. He didn't want to race, plain and simple, because he was afraid of what would happen if he did. Unlike addle-brained me, who only had a good race on my mind, Jim was concentrating on survival.

But he finally agreed, and we discussed our strategy as we tied our legs together.

Folks gathered around the field, cheering and clapping and getting a kick out of watching everybody stumble to the starting line. Mr. Lyle and Mr. Peck had brought their chairs from the storefront and pulled up nice and close, calling out our names and pointing like we were naked all over again.

The gun went off with a bang and we started out across the field, Billy tied to his cousin Marcus on our right, Luther tied to Betty Jane's big brother, Ralph, on the left. Not bad cover, but it didn't last.

Halfway across the weedy field, we were stumbling along, laughing and hanging on to each other like mad, when Ray and Arlo came zooming in around Luther and Ralph.

"Out of the way!" they hollered at Luther, who took a hard dive into the dirt with Ralph tipping over on top of him.

Now up came Ray and Arlo, out to get us, red-eyed and nearly drooling like a three-legged mad dog.

"Run!" I shouted into Jim's ear, almost picking him up off the ground to carry him.

But it was too late. We crashed into Billy and Marcus, and ended up underneath them and Mr. Mumford and his nephew Bernard. They weren't any too pleased with the situation, cursing first at Ray and Arlo, who were dashing over the finish line whooping and hollering, then at us. When Mr. Mumford sat up and saw just who'd been responsible for knocking him down, he swore bloody murder about those cursed Huns and chicken-livered folks like Mr. Morgan who called themselves Americans but wouldn't go off and fight for their country.

Jim went home after that, hardly said two words to me or Luther or Billy. I wanted to go with him, just to walk him home, but Mama made me stay to sit for the photograph she planned on sending to Papa. I wished I could write to Papa about more than just the festive doings of the day. Wished I could write about Mr. Morgan. Wished I could write that it seemed his name should have been included in the list of war casualties that Reverend Belden read.

Aunt Binny scooped up the girls and straightened their bows, then went at my hair with her comb, licking her thumb to rub a smudge off my cheek. It was pretty irritating considering I didn't think Papa would care one whit if we were to send him a picture of us all rumpled and dusty and having a good time. But Mama and Binny wanted it fancy. I looked as important and serious as I could considering Luther and Billy were across the grass making monkey faces at me the whole time I was posing.

When that was done, Mama sent me to keep a lookout on the girls while she and Binny rested in the shade.

The picnic continued, everybody but me and Luther and Billy forgetting all about poor old Jim and his daddy. Even Luther's brothers went on to have a fine time chasing the young ladies around, trying to serve up their plates and fetch lemonade for them. It was a regular comical sight, seeing those Thornton boys tipping their caps like they were proper gentlemen, puffed up with manners and falling all over themselves. We talked about smashing their faces in the fruit salad and beans, but we didn't do it. Like always, we just sat back and watched.

That's how we spent the rest of the day while we suffered through about the worst baseball game in the history of the Fourth of July. They somehow rounded up half of Mr. Motherby's shopkeeper band to play opposite Luther's brothers and a fistful of other boys. Harley made himself captain, calling up Ray and Arlo and all his friends to play the outfield and bases while he pitched. It was a slaughter, sort of like everyone was probably hoping our fight against the Germans was going to be over there in Europe. Except here the bad guys won.

"Let's get them," Billy said, that sound of daring in his voice.

"Let's," said Luther. He was starting to get some wild fire in his eyes, and I didn't like the looks of it.

"Hold on, there," I said, pushing them both back down on the bench where we were sitting. "We need to make a plan. . . ."

We didn't come up with a plan that afternoon, or during the fireworks afterwards. Though we considered all sorts of revenge, we decided that it wouldn't be fair to Jim not to include him in the action. Besides, once it got dark and the fireworks started, the town filled up with such a rousing show of patriotism that we forgot all about Harley and the others for a while. Mama and Binny and the girls went home, but she let me stay out. The boys and I hitched up with some other fellows and tossed a few firecrackers against the back wall of Jepson's until the loud boom of the town cannon signaled the end of the holiday.

Heck, that blast was so loud I bet Jim heard it too—even from way out at his place.

II

OVER THE NEXT FEW DAYS we searched through *Popular Mechanics,* and through all of our old issues of *Tip Top Weekly,* trying to come up with a scheme for revenge. We needed to figure out a clever way to get back at those Thornton boys. Billy wanted to use his Mysto Magic Set to make a potion so they'd disappear. I suggested we steal their pants and fill them with molasses. Luther thought murder was a good idea.

We talked all sorts of things around, and stewed on it for days, but as it turned out, it was Jim who came up with the plan. I think it was reading about Tarzan that did it.

"We'll booby-trap the Grove," he said.

We were sitting on his back fence, watching Mr. Morgan work one of his geldings in the corral, when Jim got this inspiration.

It was brilliant.

Naturally we had to pick the perfect time when booby-trapping would make a difference. It'd be a waste if all Harley and the boys were going to be occupied with was sitting on a log while they smoked cigars.

The answer came that night. Luther sneaked over to my house and climbed in my window to tell me the good news.

"They're taking girls there," he whispered. "They're taking Lou Anne Perkins and her friends there tomorrow night. There's a box supper at the schoolhouse for the older kids. Harley's sure to buy Lou Anne's supper. He's saved up a whole three dollars for it. And I heard him talking . . . After it's over, they're going to go to the Grove."

Luther was so excited I had to remind him to breathe.

"Harley and them'll all be off working tomorrow during the day," Luther said. "We'll be all right if we get an early start. I'll tell Billy on my way home. And we can catch up to Jim before we go to the Grove."

So next morning we set off with shovels and rakes and rope and a whole bucket of horse manure.

"What'll we do with that?" Luther wanted to know.

"Not sure yet," Jim said. "But I thought it would come in handy."

We stood around the Grove considering possibilities like setting a tiger trap in the middle of the path, or snagging branches to swing back in their faces. Billy was even willing to sacrifice his slingshot to shoot the manure from across the Grove. He said it would be like the Germans using Big Bertha to shell Paris.

But all those tricks and tactics required our presence, and though we would have taken pleasure in watching the proceedings, none of us—excepting maybe Luther—wanted an actual face-to-face encounter with his brothers.

We sat in the middle of the Grove, getting mighty depressed, sure that nothing was going to come of Jim's great idea. I took out Papa's knife and started whittling to help me think, but nothing remarkable came to mind.

Then Billy remembered the ants. "Those ants!" he said.

We looked at him like his mind had just flown away into the next county, but he said it again. "Those carpenter ants! Remember the time they came out of that log . . . ?"

Inspired. Last summer, we'd been sitting there on our same old log just doing nothing but telling whoppers, when all of a sudden Billy was covered with a swarm of inch-long disgusting black ants.

"And slugs," I said.

"And salamanders," said Luther. "We could put them all over the place where they'd sit with the girls . . ."

"Where's that going to be?" asked Jim.

We looked around and the four of us knew right off it had to be that cozy little place at the back of the Grove where three trees came together to make a sort of den. When we were little we used to pretend it was where the king's dragon lived. For the last year or so it had switched back and forth from being a gun turret to being an Allied trench, depending on the mood we were in.

I volunteered to run home and fetch some empty tins to hold our ammunition while everyone else spread the manure around and started hunting for bugs. But when I got back, they were all sitting on the log again, looking just as glum as before.

"Can't find any ants," Luther said.

"Not a single stupid slug," said Billy.

Jim shook his head. "It probably wouldn't have worked. Thanks anyway, fellows. You don't have to do nothing on my account."

No matter what Jim said, as far as the rest of us were concerned, we had to do something. It just wouldn't be right if we let all the troubles Luther's brothers put on him and his daddy go by.

That thought was mighty depressing but nobody came up with even one idea. The picture of Harley and the boys having a good time in our Grove with those girls was gnawing at all our insides as we started out for home.

"Want to go fishing?" Luther asked.

None of us did. "Think I'd better go home and help Mama beat the carpets," I said halfheartedly.

"Yeah," said Jim. "My daddy's breaking a new filly this afternoon. You all want to come over and watch?"

None of us felt like doing that either.

We didn't talk most of the way to town, kicking

stones aside, staring down at the road with our hands in our pockets. We must have looked like we'd just spent time knitting woollies with Mrs. Tilley.

"What's that smell?" Jim asked as we walked around the bend by Reverend Belden's house.

I sniffed the air.

Now, there's a big stink that comes rising up from something dead, like a cow carcass or a gutted-out old sheep. It's about the worst stink imaginable and it comes to make a human stomach turn, or at least makes a person take a step back and around on his way through the woods.

"Whatever it is, it's real dead," Billy said, holding his nose.

Jim looked at me. Then he grinned.

"Perfect," I said.

Luther caught on too. "We'll bag it," he said.

It took Billy a minute; then he figured it out. "You mean put it in the Grove?" he asked, practically hopping up and down.

Jim nodded.

We decided that what was lying by the road used to be an opossum. We covered it with the bucket so no dogs would take readily to rolling around in it; then we ran into town to pick up a burlap bag.

We stopped at the water fountain in front of Hicks's and said howdy to Mr. Lyle and Mr. Peck before we headed into the store.

Mrs. Hicks was curious when we asked her for the bag.

"What do you boys want with it?" she asked.

We told her we were planning to catch a cat later that night.

"Cats have been keeping my sisters awake," I said.

"Our dogs howl at them all night," said Luther.

Either Mrs. Hicks had had trouble with cats too, or she was a bit bloodthirsty. She wanted to know the sense in bagging a critter that she thought ought to be shot.

"Waste of a good bag," she said, shaking her head. But she gave it to us anyway, and gave us each a peach from the basket on the counter before we left. "You boys save those pits, now," she said, waving us on out of her store.

Mr. Peck and Mr. Lyle were still sitting in their chairs, but they were so deep in a discussion about the Germans staggering backwards from the Pershing Line, they didn't even notice us.

So we tore out of there, knowing it wouldn't be long before Harley and the boys were finished working. We ate our peaches, dripping the sweet juice all over our chins, glad to get the stink of that old opossum out of our noses for a few minutes. When we finished we stashed the pits in our pockets for the war effort like Mrs. Hicks told us to. Not that she had to remind us. Nobody wasted pits these days, not when they'd be put to good use making filters for the gas masks our soldiers had to wear.

We pulled straws to see who was going to hold the bag. I got the job of shoveling, which was pretty disgusting, but holding the bag meant you had to get even closer. Luther was out of the running for the job because he had such a weak stomach and we all knew if he started throwing up the rest of us probably would too.

When Billy pulled the short straw, he yanked his shirt up over his nose, pulled me by the arm, and said, "Let's get to it."

Sure would have been nice to have a couple of those gas masks just then.

The opossum's eyes were gone and its mouth was drawn back in a weird grin. It was so dead it almost fell apart when I stuck the shovel under it, and a whole platoon of maggots came squirming out of its middle. It plopped into the bag like a mud pie.

Billy tied a rope around the top of the sack, then let it out to drag behind us. All the way to the Grove we hooted and hollered, so pleased with ourselves and our great idea that we decided we needed to be there to watch the doings that night after all.

I figured them sleeping over at my house would be how we'd do it. That way Jim wouldn't have to come so far alone and Billy wouldn't have to sneak out. His mama always made him go to bed as soon as the sun went down. Probably so she could have some peace from his flying act, if you ask me.

So they ate dinner with us, all of them having a fine time teasing my sisters. Best part was I didn't have to do the dishes because I had company.

The four of us went out to play Kick the Can until it was time to go.

"Harley and them are probably playing Drop the

Hankie with those girls right now!" Billy yelled from the end of the street. "When should we go over there?"

"Before nine o'clock," Luther said. "That's when the party ends."

Since daylight savings had been thought up last March to save electricity for the war, it stayed light out so late it was hard to tell exactly what time it was. We waited for sundown, then we ducked out of the yard and headed for the Grove.

When we passed the schoolhouse we could see the party still going on.

WE HELD OUR NOSES and climbed up to take our perches. Billy and Luther and I sat up in the crook of two trees. Jim sprawled himself out on a limb, lying like a cat about to pounce.

Even from up so high and with our noses plugged we could still smell that old opossum's insides, spread out over by the den like they were. "I hope Ray steps in it first," Jim whispered.

"Naw," Luther said. "I hope it's that Lou Anne person. If she gets it stuck on her pretty little shoes . . ."

We started hooting all over again, just imagining the outcome.

Then we heard voices.

Harley and Lou Anne came strolling into the Grove in the shadowy light with their arms around each other. He was talking real coaxing in her ear. We could hear the others following—Ray and Arlo and their girls, giggling and holding hands. It was positively disgusting—almost as bad as the stink we knew they'd be coming up on in a moment or two.

"Over here, Darlin'," we heard Harley say real sweet to Lou Anne.

"Are you sure it's safe, Harley?" she asked. Then she twittered and snuggled right up to his shoulder and planted a big old kiss on his neck.

Billy had a momentary gagging spell over it and almost gave us away, but Luther clamped his hand on Billy's mouth and held him still. Sure thing, those girls all dressed in lace and ribbons, and Harley and the others wearing vests and ties and nice shoes, was a mighty sickening sight.

The happy couples were gathering below us now, the boys trying to convince the girls to follow them deeper into the Grove.

It took some words, but finally the girls agreed and Harley started leading them right straight for the den.

"Oooo, yuck!" we heard one of the girls say.

"What's that awful smell?" asked another.

"I don't smell anything," Harley said, still trying to head Lou Anne into the trees.

"I'm not taking another step over there. . . . It smells like something died. . . ."

"Aw, come on," said Ray. "It's nothing. . . ."

"Oooo!" Lou Anne shrieked. "Ooooo!" she shrieked again. Then, bull's-eye! There she went. Slipped and landed flat on her behind in that leftover opossum.

"Har-ley!" she wailed. "Take me out of here! I'm going to be . . ."

I have to say, it was pure poetry. Harley didn't even have to turn old Lou Anne upside down.

Billy gagged again, but no one heard. There was too much other retching going on down below us between those girls.

They all started bawling and as soon as Lou Anne pulled herself up off the ground, they went stumbling out of the Grove with Harley and his brothers chasing after them like puppies, pleading with them to please stop, calling out that it hadn't been their fault something had died in the Grove.

We sneaked back to my house. Billy was giggling like one of my sisters, he was so pleased with the outcome of our revenge. It did feel good, I have to admit. I felt worthy for the first time in ages; felt like Papa and the other soldiers must have felt after a victory battle, or a night raid across no-man's-land.

Luther came by the next day and told me his brothers had taken to the hills.

"Went up to gather sheep," he said. "Guess they're hiding out, staying clear of town for a few days until the girls cool off."

We had a laugh about that.

Revenge was sweet, but it didn't last long. As it turned out, the older Thornton boys must have done some thinking while they were up there bringing in those sheep. They devised another way to attack Jim and Mr. Morgan—a way that would hurt them far worse than words.

CHAPTER 12

THE DAY THE BOYS RETURNED, I had to go over to the Thortons' place to help separate the lambs from the rest of the sheep they'd brought in. Even before I got there, I heard Harley yelling.

"I'm not doing it!" he was shouting at Luther. "I'm not about to drive no slacker's sheep to market. It's bad enough we sheared and gathered for him."

I wasn't sure how Jim's daddy was going to take such bad news, being dependent on the rest of us and the Thorntons' dogs the way he was.

"How are they supposed to make it over the winter without selling their sheep?" Luther asked.

"Let Morgan worry about it," Harley said. "Maybe if he does, he'll give a thought to our daddies over there, fighting the Germans. Let him worry just how *we're* supposed to get through another winter without *them*!"

I went back home that afternoon needing to talk with Mama. She appreciated it when I brought my troubles to her, even though she usually offered me the same advice each time, mainly, "Do whatever you think is right, Joe. Do what your papa would do."

How she thought I knew what that was, I can't imagine. I sure wished I could write and ask Papa. I'd tell him how lousy I thought the whole situation with the Thorntons was, and how rotten they were treating Mr. Morgan just because he'd decided to stay home where he belonged.

Binny and the girls had gone berry picking, and Mama and I were setting the table outdoors for dinner. This was Papa's favorite way to take a meal, out in the fresh air, with the evening light shining off the edges of the trees and the birds singing to each other. I guessed Mama was missing him especially bad, since his regular weekly letter hadn't come yet. I was following behind Mama, laying silverware on top of the folded napkins, when I told her what Harley had said.

"Shame," Mama said. "Shame, shame, shame."

I wasn't sure right off if she was calling shame on Harley, or shame on Mr. Morgan, or just shame on the whole terrible situation.

"I can't imagine what they'll do if they can't get their sheep to the auction," she said. "I don't suppose anyone in town is going to be too ready to help the Morgans this year. You know, Joe, even if Harley did take those sheep along, there's a chance nobody would buy them."

This thought hadn't occurred to me, but if Harley and the folks at the picnic were an example of how the rest of the county felt about men like Mr. Morgan—no matter why they'd chosen not to go to war—she might just have a point.

"What should we do about it?" I asked.

"I don't see that we can do anything," Mama said, shaking her head. "We need Harley and the boys and if we make a fuss, they're liable to refuse to take *our* sheep. I can't think past that, Joe. Without your father here, and all you children to feed and look after, how can we risk it?"

"What about Jim, Mama? What'll I tell him?"

"Do whatever you think is right, Joe. Do what your papa would do." There it was, right between the forks and spoons. I went inside, brought out the chairs, and set them around the table.

After Binny and the girls returned we ate, with wasps buzzing around the chicken pie that Mama'd made. We sat there late, talking and eating slowly, the white linen tablecloth flapping in the breeze while the shadows pulled out long around the yard and the day cooled into evening. For dessert, Alice brought the bottle of cream from the ice box and we poured it over our fresh berries.

We wrote letters to Papa that night. I told him everything was fine. But it gnawed at me. Made me feel like I was being dishonest. What I really wanted to say was that I thought we'd probably all be a lot better off if he'd come back home.

AFTER CHORES THE NEXT MORNING, Mama put me to work making extra kindling so she could keep the fire going all day. It was time to start "putting up." She and Binny were going to be making early jam.

By ten o'clock the kitchen was like an oven, jars boiling on the back of the stove, paraffin melting in a tin to the side, and up front a big pot of bubbling fruit that Binny stirred while she sang.

That jam was making the kitchen smell mighty sweet, even though this year we couldn't use much sugar since such a big share went to the soldiers. The girls and I stood around eating berries and licking spoons until Mama finally decided Binny was all the help she could tolerate and she'd about tired of having all of us underfoot.

"Go on, now," she said. "Run to the store. I need another box of paraffin. Mr. Jepson will have it in his back room, so you'll have to ask for it. And, Joe, put those books and magazines I collected for the soldiers in the wagon. Take them down and put them in the bin outside the library, please." She paused and turned to look at me. "And see if a letter's come from your father."

The girls skipped and sang all the way there. I walked as far behind them as I could, scanning the streets for a sign of Luther's brothers. I pulled the wagon of books along, then stopped to drop them in the donation box outside the library. Both girls hopped in the wagon and made me pull them the rest of the way.

When we got to Jepson's, Helen ran ahead to the counter.

I could tell by the downturned look on Mr. Jepson's

face that no letter had come from Papa. Poor Mr. Jepson must have felt some responsibility for the bad news, either that or it bothered him to be disappointing a six-year-old.

He took Helen's hand. "Now, now," he said. "A week's not so long between letters. You'll hear from him soon, Miss Farrington. Paper says Lloyd George promises victory's not far away."

I was sure Helen didn't have the first idea who Lloyd George was. She turned and walked back down the aisle to me and Alice with a mighty confused look on her face.

"But the Sears Roebuck catalog came," Mr. Jepson called to her cheerfully. Helen spun around like a top and ran back to him. You'd have thought he'd just turned into Santa Claus the way she giggled and fussed when he gave the catalog to her. I sent the girls outside with it to sit on the bench and wait for me.

"I'd like a box of paraffin, please," I told Mr. Jepson.

"I'm certain you'll hear from your father soon," he said. "I'm sure he's just fine. Mail from the front can be very, very slow, you know."

I nodded, wondering why the mail should be any slower this week than it was the last. Mr. Jepson went off into the back room, muttering something about slow mail delivery and needlessly worrying folks.

Funny. I hadn't been particularly worried at all, until he mentioned I ought to be.

He came back and put the box of paraffin on the counter. "So you're helping your mother put up this year? And helping to look after your sisters? What a fine young man, Joseph. What a fine, helpful young man."

Even though I wished I was being praised for something a bit more heroic than helping Mama make jam, taking his compliment felt pretty good. I said thank you, gave him money for the paraffin, and went out to meet up with the girls.

I was just stepping through the door when I noticed Mrs. Morgan and Claire coming out of Hicks's across the street. Claire was wearing a blue ribbon in her hair and looking as beautiful as ever. I gathered my composure, pretending I didn't notice.

Alice and Helen were on the bench out front, the catalog open on their laps. But they weren't looking at it. Both of them were staring at Claire and her mother. Alice turned as I came out the door.

"What's the matter?" I asked.

Alice glanced back at the Morgans as they disappeared around the corner at the end of the block. Helen crawled over Alice's lap and started to say something, but Alice reached out and covered her mouth.

"Nothing," she said, getting up to pull the wagon. "Let's go."

We were almost home and heading past the schoolhouse before Alice told me what had gone wrong outside the store.

"Those ladies came by," she said, letting Helen skip ahead of us. "Mrs. Tilley and Mabel Dawes. Claire and her mama came by too and stopped to say hello to us." Alice looked up at me. "I wasn't wrong to say hello back to them, was I, Joe?"

"No," I said. "Why would that be wrong? What happened?"

Helen turned around and hopped back to us. "Mrs. Tilley told us Mama was bad," she said, taking Alice by the hand.

Alice went on. "Mrs. Morgan was talking to us. She told Helen she liked her hat. Then Claire asked me if I had fun at the Fourth of July picnic. That's all." She hesitated, looking up at me, her face stricken.

"That's not all," I said. "There's more. Tell me."

"Mrs. Tilley scolded us for talking to the Morgans."

Helen yanked on Alice's arm. "Tell him what she said."

"She said Mama was doing a poor job by letting you be friends with Jim. And that Papa would be mighty angry if he knew we were speaking to the Morgans. She said it right in front of Claire and her mother, Joe. Right in front of them."

"And she was shaking her finger like an old witch too," Helen said. "I don't like Mrs. Tilley anymore. What's the matter with speaking to Claire? Mrs. Morgan liked my hat."

"Let's go," I said. "Mama will be wanting the paraffin. And don't worry about speaking to the Morgans. You go right ahead if you want to. I'm sure Papa wouldn't mind at all."

"What about Mrs. Tilley?" Helen asked. "Do I have to speak to her too?"

"To be polite," I said. "Only to be polite."

I thought it was pretty curious what the war had done to Mrs. Tilley. I suppose it had done strange things to a lot of people's way of thinking. But just then, it gave me pleasure to know that as far as I could tell, what I had said to Helen was exactly what Papa would have wanted me to say.

Before we reached home I told the girls not to mention to Mama what had happened with Mrs. Tilley. "No use upsetting her," I said. "She'll be worried enough that there was no letter from Papa."

But I told her anyway. It just didn't seem right not to. Fortunately, Binny had gone upstairs to nap.

Mama turned from the stove and wiped her forehead with the back of her hand. "What are you saying, Joseph? That Mrs. Tilley told the girls they shouldn't speak—"

Alice interrupted. "She said Papa would disapprove if he knew we were speaking to the Morgans. That isn't right, is it Mama?"

My mother pushed the pot of boiling jam to the back of the stove, then reached up to the stovepipe and turned down the damper.

"It most certainly is not," she said. Her voice sounded stiff, angry. "Get dressed, girls. Do it quietly. Don't wake Binny. Joe, put on a clean shirt. We're going to make a call."

Half an hour later we were all outside, climbing into the Hudson, Mama wearing the hat Papa liked, the girls brushed and combed and wearing fresh ribbons, me holding two warm jars of jam.

"Where are we going?" asked Alice.

"Are we going to tell Mrs. Tilley to mind her own business?" Helen asked.

Mama turned around in her seat and frowned at Helen. "No such thing," she said. "We are just going calling. That's all. Sit up straight and mind your manners."

Mama drove us smack-dab through the middle of town, drove us slowly, and waved when she saw Mr. Lyle and Mr. Peck outside the feedstore. Waved when we passed Mr. and Mrs. Higgins. And waved in a friendly manner to Mrs. Tilley, who was just walking into her yard.

When we turned left at the end of Main Street I knew she was taking us over to visit the Morgans. And so did everybody else in town.

Claire came out to greet us on the front porch.

"Papa's gone to the far pasture to see about a sick horse," she said. "But Mama's inside, if you'd like to come in."

Mama thanked her and went through the open door.

"Jim's out back if you want to go see him, Joe," Claire said, looking straight at me and smiling like an angel when I handed her the jam. "I'll take the girls upstairs with me."

"Sure," I said, feeling my voice stick like glue in my throat.

I stood there till the door closed and stayed to listen to her footsteps disappear down their front hall. Then I went around back to find Jim. I thought it was a good chance for me to discuss his Harley predicament.

"Doesn't matter to me if Harley takes our sheep or not," Jim said when I mentioned it. "We'll be fine."

"Does that mean you're not going to ride the drive

with us?" I asked. "We need you. That darned dog Spit is worthless. She's not about to listen to me."

"Don't think it's wise that I do, what with everyone feeling so bad about my daddy."

"But we always do the drive together," I said. "Since we were little kids." Ever since we could sit on a horse, we'd all gone along, pretending to be old-time cowpokes, pushing our herd across the plains to Denver or Abilene. Jim was our partner, and deep down I was just coming to realize that if Jim didn't go with us, Harley and the boys would have succeeded in breaking us up.

"Hey, Jim," I said, taking him by the arm. "You don't go, I don't go."

He turned around and looked kind of solemn at me, like I'd pushed him into a place where his mind got stuck.

"What?" he asked.

"I said, if you don't go on the drive, I'm not going either."

"Don't be dumb. You have to. Harley won't take your sheep if you don't help."

"Who says?"

"Harley'll say that. You go on. Don't worry about me. My daddy'd be upset with me if I went anyway."

"But it won't be the same without you. What'll we do for laughs?"

"Those fellows will only hound me if I go," Jim said, picking a long stem of grass and chewing on it.

"Or call you chicken if you don't."

I didn't mean it, really I didn't. It just slipped out all by itself.

"You'd call me that?"

"Heck, no," I said, most grateful for a chance to pull my foot out of my mouth. "And if anybody did I'd cream them. Anybody but Luther's brothers, that is."

Jim grinned at me.

"Aw, come on," I said. "You're going to miss out on a good time. It isn't fair of your daddy to keep you home just because they aren't taking your sheep. We can have fun anyhow."

Jim considered this for longer than he usually considered things. But I suppose it was an important decision.

In the end, he decided to go with us.

CHAPTER 13

HARLEY WAS FUMING. He was so mad I was afraid his hair was going to catch fire.

At first I thought it was just because his dog, Ben, had met up with a porcupine and couldn't see good enough to work the drive. But that wasn't it.

"That Morgan runt's going? Is that what you're telling me?" Harley paced up and down the fence, hollering at Luther.

It was dawn and we were waiting for Jim. None of us had thought to make a special announcement that he was coming along—it didn't even occur to us. Jim had always been part of the drive before.

"We're down a dog, so I suppose we could use the help," Harley grumbled. "But he's staying at the back eating dust if he's coming. I don't want to hear him or see him. You understand?"

Luther nodded. Billy and I did too.

"And if Ray picks a fight with him, so be it. I'm not

stepping in for anybody this time. We've got sheep to move and work to do. If any of you babies need wet-nursing, I'm leaving you on the trail."

We weren't driving all our sheep into Maxwell, just the lambs and a few old ewes we wanted to sell, but there were still hundreds of them. Their bawling kicked up quite a racket and was a pleasant distraction from Harley's pacing. Finally, Jim came galloping down the road and pulled his horse up at the gate.

Harley didn't say so much as a howdy-do to him. He shook his head, opened the gate, and sent the dogs in after the sheep. Then he climbed onto his horse and yanked it around hard to head out in front of us.

Those sheep came through the gate hell-bent for the open and scattering in all directions without any regard for who was trying to lead the way. So we were off, whooping and yipping at them to bunch them back onto the road. Sheep are a whole lot stupider than cattle. Cattle will mosey along fine without panicking and splitting off of their own mind. They kick up more dust but they're sure easier to work than sheep.

But we were going to be great. We were going to get those sheep to Maxwell without a hitch, and show Harley and the others we were the best drovers in the valley.

Spit wasn't taking orders, but she was doing fine keeping track of her side of the flock, while Luther's dog, Pete, worked the other. The big boys took up the head of the line, while the rest of us were doing the driving from behind.

"You got it handled over there?" I called to Billy as a car came up the hill behind us. He was moving back and forth like he was supposed to, easing the sheep along at a careful distance. Luther and Jim had swung left and right, keeping track of any strays that might decide to take off into the brush. The car moved slowly through the flock. Thankfully, whoever was driving was polite enough not to honk and send those sheep into a flutter.

It was a fair day, with just a little spatter of high clouds, enough so the sun wouldn't burn down on us like a furnace. I usually liked taking the sheep to town, but riding back there I suddenly got to thinking about Papa, missing him way down like I did when he first left.

I might have become accustomed to going through a regular day without him, but I'd never get used to thinking about how far away he was. How I couldn't reach him, or call out to him. And how this drive was going to be different from all the others I'd been on. How this year, after the drive was over, there wouldn't be a picnic. And how right now, while he was off someplace in Europe, I was following Harley instead of him, and Mr. Morgan wasn't even there to keep the Thornton boys in line.

I think we all felt it, because we didn't talk for ages—just moved those sheep up the road, eating dust, and wondering if we'd be doing the same thing without our daddies next year.

That's the only explanation I have for what happened. All of us must have been distracted at the same time, gazing off over all those white rumps, dozing with the rhythm of the saddle, our minds off somewhere in France.

It started when Billy's mare shied away from a clump of boulders at the edge of the road. She made a quick zigzag step, then jerked ahead a few paces, almost bucking Billy off. He swore and righted himself, but was so irritated with his horse he gave her a hard jab in the sides to get her going straight again.

Wrong thing to do. Billy ought to have known better than to kick his horse when she was already skittish.

She nearly bolted right out from under him.

Billy hauled back on the reins, but that horse was so jittery she just kept charging forward, right straight into the middle of that pack of sheep.

Sure enough, a nervous horse will do unpredictable things, but you ought to see what that many sheep will do when *they're* surprised.

In a matter of seconds we had sheep going in fifty different directions, leaping ditches and flying off into the gullies on either side of the road. They scattered into the brush, then ran back down the road past me, in completely the wrong direction.

It was a genuine straight-from-the-devil nightmare.

We started shouting and calling to the dogs to come help. I ripped around and caught up with the wayward lambs that had run behind me. Luther took off into the brush, hollering cuss words that would have shamed his daddy. Jim went down the other side, into a steep draw filled with thistles.

When Harley got wind of what was happening, he galloped back down the line to help Luther round up his strays. Billy saw Ray and Arlo coming our way and steered his lurchy horse down the hill toward Jim. Ray was swearing worse than Luther, but stopped long enough to tell Arlo to come over and help me keep the ones in back bunched together.

Pretty soon, Harley rode out of the brush with Luther and about fifty sheep. Without a hitch, he eased them in alongside the others, and it looked like we were back in business.

But then, here came Jim and Billy roaring up the hill with their thirty or forty. They hit the road way too fast and headed those strays right into the side of the flock. This time the sheep split my way and all hell broke loose. They turned a good one-eighty degrees and started making a beeline back down the road at a gallop.

Harley was out of his mind with rage by now. He spurred his horse and went charging down the line hollering like he was ready to explode. Luther was so surprised he just sat there looking stupid as those sheep streamed by on either side of him. But the way all the rest of us were chasing those animals around we must have looked like the Keystone Kops.

Ray went crazy. He rode over between Jim and Billy and yanked them both off their horses with one swift jerk. It was amazing to watch, two mid-grown boys hanging one from each of Ray's arms as he dragged them off the road. He dumped them there in the dust by me, then went back for their horses.

"What's he doing?" Billy shouted through the riot of sheep commotion as he scrambled to his feet.

Ray leaned over and grabbed the reins on Billy's and Jim's horses.

"Hey! What are you doing taking our horses?" Billy yelled after him.

Ray pulled up sharp and turned around.

"You two are on foot from here," he sneered. "You're way too dangerous on horseback."

With that he led those ponies away and rode off toward the front of the line.

Arlo and Harley, meantime, had succeeded in bringing the situation under control and all the sheep were headed in the same direction again.

Jim stood and brushed the dust off. "I guess we're walking, then," he said matter-of-factly. "How far do you suppose it is?"

"I don't know," I said. "About five more miles, I gather. You can split between me and Luther riding double."

Didn't take any of us long to realize that this was going to be the worst part. Positively mortifying, in fact. Us red-hot drovers, riding double because the big boys took our horses away.

But that's what we did, like little kids, two to a horse and saddle-sore, trying to move those lousy sheep over the hill.

"Hey, Bucko!" Billy's cousin Lou yelled as we rode into Maxwell.

"Harley Thornton!" Mr. Finklemeyer's son called from the corner as we passed. "See you brought the little boys to help!"

We rode all the way to the stockyard with the whole dang town coming out to wave and snicker at us. Dishonor and humiliation weren't words harsh enough for how rotten and angry we were feeling. I was just grateful Papa wasn't there to see. But you'd probably have had to be as far away as France not to hear about it once the news got out.

CHAPTER 14

AFTER THE FIASCO of making complete fools of ourselves on the drive, we stayed clear of each other for a few days. Jim's daddy was displeased with him for going along in the first place—said he thought Jim had more sense than to go against his *own* sensibilities. I guess Jim was trying to make it up to him by staying close to home and helping with the horses. I, for one, was too sore to do much of anything after that ride with him.

Billy's grandma Patsy was having a birthday, so he and his mama left for Maxwell to see her. And as for Luther . . . well, let's just say his shame was so great at having the rest of us as friends that for the time being he was going to make peace with Harley and the others.

That left me with Mama and the girls, and Aunt Binny, of course.

I think Binny being with us for so long was finally

taking a toll on Mama, because one afternoon she declared that we were due for a holiday.

"We're going to the beach," she said. "We'll pack a picnic and drive out to the ocean. Does that sound all right with you, Joe?"

The beach sounded like the best idea anyone had had in ages. We hadn't been there since last year when we celebrated Papa's birthday.

Aunt Binny set to filling the picnic hamper. She made three kinds of sandwiches and a hurry-up cake with boiled frosting. I helped gather blankets and sunhats and buckets and shovels. Binny complained that sitting on the sand would cause her bowels to freeze up, so I carried a kitchen chair outside too and shoved it into the car.

The ride to the ocean was a fine time. Binny and the girls sat in the back seat and Mama let me drive. The Hudson was a grand car, and I felt honored to be sitting up there in Papa's seat, steering us down the road, the man of the family once again. It felt a far cry better than riding double through Maxwell with Jim behind me on that horse.

Binny wasn't so sure. She was as old-fashioned about automobiles as about indoor toilets, I suppose. She grumbled, saying she'd read in *Sunset* magazine that "excessive driving leads to indigestion, blood pressure, brain fag, and fatty degeneration." I wouldn't have said it aloud to her face, but it seemed from her description that she must have done a fair amount of driving around in cars herself.

The girls squealed when we came around the bend and caught our first glimpse of the ocean: a bluish-green triangle between the hills, with a thin bank of fog hanging just above it.

Our beach wasn't a sunny one; we were too far north for that. It was a rugged, windy, storm-scarred place—full of history and tragedy. Some folks said there was an ancient Spanish treasure buried in a secret cave out there. Papa'd told us that when he was a boy he and his friends had gone looking for it. But no one ever found the cave, much less any gold doubloons. I was thinking just then that it sure would have been nice if gold doubloons were what Papa'd hidden in that old cookie tin he'd buried so long ago. Heck, if that was the case, that tin might be worth looking for after all.

Aunt Binny and the girls all stood up and took hold of the front seat, bobbing up and down and pushing each other for the best view. Once we saw it full-on, we were practically up on the beach, the wind floating Mama's hair in little wisps around her face. It made her laugh.

One thing about living on the West Coast came clear to me as we pulled up onto the sand. It was an idea that had never occurred to me before. My father and so many other fathers were "across the ocean," as we always said, fighting somewhere in Europe. But it was the wrong ocean, an ocean so far away I couldn't imagine it. As I looked out over that big Pacific, waves thundering on the beach like artillery fire, it felt to me like

Papa was a million miles away and that I had made a mistake driving to this ocean, that I ought to have been heading in the other direction, toward the Atlantic.

Mama climbed out and put the girls in order, loading them down with baskets and buckets and blankets. I grabbed Binny's chair while she took charge of keeping sand out of the food. Then I held Mama's arm the way Papa always did and escorted her to the water.

"Take off your shoes, Mama!" Alice sang out. "Run in the waves!"

Mama let go of my arm. "Come on, Joe. Let's run together, like we did last year with Papa."

We sat down and slipped off our shoes, while Aunt Binny fussed about the wind and blowing sand.

"It will ruin the cake," Binny said. "This wind will ruin the cake!"

"Oh, phooey on the cake," Mama replied, laughing as she took my hand. "Really, Binny, we came to the beach to have fun!"

Mama and I ran to the water then, holding hands and letting the waves splash up on our knees. My sisters got a huge kick out of seeing Mama act so silly, and they danced around, nudging me out of the way. But that was all right. Mama seemed happy for the first time in months.

We built castles and dug moats and ate our sandwiches and gritty cake, then buried Aunt Binny in the sand when she finally relaxed. She decided she liked the beach and didn't mind the wind so much after all, so she took the girls and went skipping off to look for seashells.

Mama packed the leftovers into the basket; then she and I stood together and watched the waves break over the rocks out on the point, both of us with Papa on our minds but not saying so.

When the fog started to roll our way, we built a big fire and the two of us wrapped up in blankets.

"It's been a good day, hasn't it, Joe?" Mama said.

"Yes," I answered. "It's been just fine."

"I used to come here as a girl, you know? First with my family, then with your father. He's partial to watching the sea. Do you remember that about him?"

"Yes, I remember."

About then, Alice came running up the beach shouting, "Look what we found! Look what we found!"

Aunt Binny was trudging behind her, Helen waving and jumping at her side. Aunt Binny had something in her hand.

"Goodness, Binny!" Mama said, tossing aside the blanket and pulling herself up off the sand. "What on earth do you have there?"

"It's a starfish!" Alice cried.

"A purple starfish!" said Helen.

Aunt Binny looked put-upon, holding that creature as far out in front of her as she could. "The girls insisted I bring it to show you," she said with dismay in her voice.

"I found it," Helen said.

"Did not," said Alice.

"I saw it first," protested Helen. "I saw it but I didn't say anything."

"Is it alive?" Mama asked, moving in for a closer look.

"I don't believe so," Binny said. "It doesn't smell very alive."

It didn't, she was right. In fact, that old starfish stunk. But the girls were so excited they didn't care, and because they were excited Mama agreed that they could bring it home. "As long as you keep it out in the yard," she said.

We packed up and started for home, all laughing and singing songs over the stench of that dead purple starfish.

We were almost to town when Reverend and Mrs. Belden met us on the road.

Now normally, the proper driving behavior is to pull off to the side and yield to whoever has the most difficult pass or the most unruly vehicle. Move out of the way is the general rule.

But here came the Beldens, barreling down the road in their new Stutz Bearcat, their horn *ah-ooo-gah*ing away at us. That car might have done a fine job at the Indianapolis 500, but it was going way too fast for that narrow road. It was most unusual, and at first Mama grabbed my arm, saying she wondered if perhaps the reverend had lost control.

"Stop!" the reverend was shouting. "Whoa!"

"What?" Mama cried out. "Does he think he's got runaway horses? He's driving an *automobile,* for Heaven's sake!"

Aunt Binny was standing up behind us now. "Get off the road, Joe! Let them by or they'll run us down!"

I found a narrow spot by the side of the road and came to a lurchy stop.

The Beldens started waving to us. I was thinking it was a thank-you wave, but it wasn't. And their car hadn't been running out of control. They'd just been in a big fat hurry to find Mama. Mrs. Belden had a telegram in her hand.

CHAPTER 15

It said Papa had gone missing in France.

I discovered that day that true bad news travels lots faster than gossip. By the time we got home folks were already gathered outside our house ready to jump us and offer condolences.

Luther was there, with his mama. Even his brothers showed up. Mrs. Thornton had made us food.

"Oh, Joe," Mama said as I helped her from the car. "Do tell them to go home, would you? Be polite. Thank them for coming. . . ."

Mama's voice quavered but she didn't break down.

"Alice, you and Helen come inside and wash up. Binny, be a dear, help Joe with our guests. . . ."

Luther was looking as sour in the face as my stomach was feeling. "Sorry," he said, soft, before he looked away.

His mama handed me the pan of salmon cakes she'd made. "Ring us up, Joseph," she said. "If there's anything we can do."

I said thank you to them while Binny assured every-one else that we'd hear good news about Papa soon. For all her daily fussing and need for Lydia E. Pinkham tablets, Binny was a rock that afternoon. Straight and strong and as cheerful and friendly as a person could be under such lousy circumstances.

While Alice and I made dinner and Binny played with Helen, Mama rested in her chair. It was as if the bad news had sucked all the life out of my mother, as if she'd sent herself off somewhere else and was watching the rest of us from far away.

Beside me in the kitchen, Alice suddenly seemed a lot older than nine. She stepped right into the job of putting dinner on the table. Neither of us could stom-ach the thought of Mrs. Thornton's salmon cakes, so she made milk toast. Which was fine, since no one had much of an appetite anyway.

With Papa so hard on our minds, a quiet came down on the house—one that even Binny couldn't think of how to fill. She tried, by telling us the story of "The Murders in the Rue Morgue," thinking a little fright might distract us, I guess. But it didn't.

We all went to bed early.

Spit followed Mama upstairs. Have to give that dog some credit. She stuck so close to Mama you could tell she knew something had gone wrong.

That night I came to understand that in some ways, "gone missing" is much worse than "dead." With "dead" you know what to expect, and other folks know how to behave. They cry and say how sorry they are. And you cry and tell them things like "He's at peace in

Heaven," or "God rest his soul." They send the coffin home with a flag draped over it, and everyone comes to the funeral with flowers.

I knew about funerals because of Andy Marble's. Everyone went to that. It was all a very sad affair, but at least it had an ending that didn't leave you wondering.

Wondering was all we had and it started up fierce with me. I wondered all night long, staring at the shadows floating on my ceiling, imagining all sorts of things that might have happened to Papa, and privately hating President Wilson and that faraway place called France.

All the bad things I'd seen and read about in the papers, all the photographs of the war, all those stories people told about how Germans were eating Belgian babies—every awful thing came pouring down on me. But most of all it was Papa I saw in my mind. And I started feeling a hurt growing inside me—a hurt I knew was anger at him for leaving us all behind.

I stayed home with the girls for the next few days. We dusted the house and put so much wax on the furniture the whole place smelled like a lemon orchard. Mama and Binny cooked and cooked some more, and I washed all the downstairs windows.

The rest of the time I played with Alice and Helen, being Jailbreak Joe of course, and without complaining. I turned the jumprope for them when they asked, built them a seesaw out of some boards and an old tree stump, and tried to teach them how to play marbles.

They ran a short article about Papa in the paper, and

put his name on the casualty list under "missing in action." Even so, the next day Mama sat us all down to write to him like always.

I'd just finished my letter when someone knocked at the front door. "Get that, will you, Joe?" Mama said. "I'm not up to company. Take a calling card."

I went to the door expecting to find either Mrs. Tilley or Mrs. Belden with an armload of baked goods. But it was Luther.

"What the heck are you knocking for?" I asked. Luther'd never knocked before in his life. Come to think of it, I'm pretty sure he'd never used the front door before either.

"Mama told me I shouldn't come," he said. "She said you wouldn't want to go anywhere just yet, what with your daddy missing . . ."

"Hello there, Luther," Mama called from the other room. "Won't you come in? Would you like some cake?"

"No, thank you, Mrs. Farrington. I didn't mean to disturb you."

"I suppose you came by to collect Joe. He's finished his chores. There's no sense in him staying here. Take him with you if you like."

Luther said we could go swimming since he figured his brothers might take pity on my sorry situation and leave us alone for once. Funny thing. The business with Harley and the boys suddenly didn't seem so important or worrisome—what with the bigger worry of Papa on my mind.

But I didn't say that to Luther. I grabbed my bathing

suit and we headed for the swimming hole, where we were supposed to meet Billy and Jim.

It was good getting out with Luther. But it didn't take him any time to jump right in with questions.

"Where'd your daddy go missing?" he asked.

"Not sure," I said. "Someplace in France."

"Do you think he's captured?"

"Don't know that either," I said. "Don't know much of anything except he's missing."

"Golly, maybe he's got amnesia and can't remember who he is."

"Could be. I suppose it'd be better than being dead, wouldn't it?"

Luther didn't answer, probably tossing the idea of "dead" around in his head, considering if he ought to ask me if I thought my Papa was. He opted not to speak anymore about it.

Walking along, folks passed like they always did, but now they tipped their hats and raised a hand to say hello. Just because my daddy was missing, all of a sudden I was a celebrity. Folks are queer that way, pointing you out just when you don't want to be recognized for fear you'll bust out crying, calling attention to you just when you want to go hide under a rock.

They were all well-meaning, not like when they pointed at Jim or Mr. Morgan or at us boys running naked through town. But somehow I felt it was sort of the same. Folks like to get involved in other people's business and drama. I could have spent the rest of my life walking down that road without a soul saying a word to me, but give me a parcel of trouble and all of a sudden I'm a big shot. It was a hell of a way to get respect.

Billy and Jim were already in the water when we got there. It was hot out and we didn't take but two minutes to put on our bathing suits and join them. I jumped in and swam over to the rocks on the other side of the river.

Billy paddled over and bopped me on the head. "Hey there, Joe! How you doing?"

I splashed him hard and he dunked me; then Luther came diving in to join the fun. Jim raced over and made a sloppy wake with his wild kicking and bad arm strokes, flailing away in the water like a threshing machine.

We made so much commotion we probably scared all the fish for miles around. But it was a good time, and I felt easy there with all of them, doing regular stuff with plenty of space around me so I could get Papa off my mind.

By the time we climbed out and sat on the rocks to dry off, everyone was beginning to feel relaxed enough to start inquiring about my tragic circumstances. Billy went first.

"Bet you feel pretty bad about your daddy, don't you, Joe?"

"Real bad," I said, leaning to put all my might into skipping a rock as far as I could over the water.

I think they were all curious about what it was like to have a father who'd gone missing. But it was a feeling I couldn't put into words, so I didn't try.

"Pa says it's a real shame any of your daddies went

131

over there at all," said Jim. "He says war's a shame all the way around."

When I looked at him, I felt almost sick. Suddenly I didn't care one whit what his father thought. How could Mr. Morgan even have an opinion on the subject?

"Yeah," said Billy. "But everyone's got to make sacrifices. It's a noble thing to die over there fighting the Germans."

"My daddy's not dead," I reminded him. "He's just missing."

Then Luther spoke up. "Harley says it's an honor to fight for your country. He says we ought to feel proud that our daddies are over there."

"How does Harley know honor from nothing, Luther? He's as bad as Jim here, who has a daddy who won't even fight."

I stood up and dove into the water, swimming hard, letting all my anger out. Anger at them. Anger at Papa for going away. It felt good, slapping and kicking like I could beat all the sadness out of the world, and screaming to myself underwater where no one could hear.

A while later, Jim asked us over for lemonade. He was trying to smooth things over between us, trying to make it up with me, I suppose. So we walked on over there.

I could see Jim's daddy as we passed the field in front of his house. He was with his horses, and had his back to us. I watched him lean down to lift up one of the horse's hooves, and I kept watching as he checked it, put it back down, stood up, and rubbed the horse on the neck.

My stomach started to hurt just then, like it was growing a big rotten hole in it.

"I'd better get home," I said. "Mama might be needing me."

I didn't wait for the boys to try to stop me. I just turned away from them and Mr. Morgan there so happy in that field with his horses, and ran all the way to my house. I took the back way around town so I wouldn't have to see anyone staring at me, or pass that poster of the soldier in Jepson's window.

That night Aunt Binny took me aside and said I ought to stay close to home for a few more days, to help Mama through the hard time. She didn't realize that I would be just as glad to hang around the house trying on dresses for Mama and sweeping the kitchen three times a day. I didn't want to go out. Didn't want to see anybody. Didn't want to see Jim.

I lay in bed that night, some part of me wishing it was Mr. Morgan lost in France, and wondering like always about Papa—wondering if he was safe, wondering what I could do. Sure thing, a whole year of beefless Tuesdays, a million buckets of peach pits, and all the war bonds in the world were not going to find him and bring him back to us.

That's when I started thinking about the box.

I dreamed about it, imagined it, wondered what was inside.

The next morning I couldn't get it off my mind and decided to go up the hill to our place by the cypress trees to think about it.

When I climbed the hill I realized I hadn't been there since that last evening with Papa. It felt strange going alone, and even more strange sitting down on my rock with no one on the other one to talk to. I wondered if Papa'd ever be there with me again. His whittling scraps were still on the ground, scattered in the grass by my feet.

I looked out over the valley, over our yard and the river in the distance. In the winter you can see the bridge from up there, but in summer the trees are all bloomed out so it's hidden. In the other direction, on clear days, you can see the ocean between the hills where they come together at the mouth of the river.

How could we have been dancing around in the waves, singing and having a jolly old time while the whole town was out hunting for us to give us the bad news? There we were splashing and laughing, not even knowing Papa had gone missing way over in France.

A sharp wind came up the hill, bending the grass back against the ground. Where *was* that box? Papa's lost treasure. Hidden for years and years. Maybe if I found it, it would help somehow. Maybe if I could find the box, whoever was looking for Papa could find him.

16

I WENT ALONE, with only a shovel, and walked through town with Papa on my mind. I explored places he said he'd roamed as a boy, hoping I could find *something* that would make sense of what was happening.

I tried to imagine what sort of boy he had been, with so many brothers and all. I wanted to know what part of him he'd valued so much he had to keep it hidden from them. They couldn't have been anything like Luther's brothers, I was sure of that, but all the same, they must have tormented him some.

I don't know what I was thinking—believing I'd just walk out and start digging up the countryside without a plan. But that's what I did. I became a digging fool, making holes anywhere I could think that Papa might have been.

Spit snuck up on me one day and made a real nuisance of herself, sniffing around my shovel as if I was having a bone-digging party, kicking up dirt all over the place. That's not why I booted her off the job, though. I sent her away because I didn't want any company.

I wanted to be by myself. And for a time, looking for that box kept me away from the other fellows. Luther came by the house once or twice to try to coax me into goofing around with them, but I told him Mama wanted me for chores. I know Luther probably thought I had come down with some mental disease, wanting to do chores instead of taking off with him for fun. But he wouldn't have understood if I'd tried to tell him the real truth—that I didn't want to talk about my father, and I didn't want to be around Jim.

That feeling got worse the day Mama sent me over to Luther's to return Mrs. Thornton's pan.

Luther met me at the door. "Hey, Joe, where've you been? How come you don't want to go to the river with us anymore?"

"Never said I didn't want to," I told him on the way to the kitchen.

"Then why don't you come? We're going fishing this afternoon."

Harley and Ray were in the kitchen with Mrs. Thornton.

"My mama sent this over for you, Mrs. Thornton," I said, holding out the pan. "She said to say it was a big help."

"Set it on the table there by Harley," she answered, wiping her hands on her apron and coming over to me. "Your poor mama. Now, I told her I didn't need this back right away. You thank her, will you, Joseph?

And tell her we're all thinking about her and praying for your daddy."

Harley put down his fork and turned around to look at me. "It's a rotten shame about your daddy, Joe. Doggone stinking shame."

Maybe Harley was trying to be nice, but it still felt crummy. Gaining *his* respect just because Papa'd gone missing was worse than seeing all those sympathetic folks in town nodding at me. Especially when I knew that a few days before, Harley'd as soon smack me in the head with a tomato as wish me howdy-do.

"You got to be proud," he went on. "You got to be proud having a daddy who's such a good soldier."

I knew Papa was probably a good soldier—a brave soldier—but I was reasonably sure getting lost wasn't what he'd intended to do when he went off to fight in the war. And I knew being proud was the last thing on *my* mind. All I wanted was for Papa to come back home.

"Yeah," said Ray. "Not like some folks we know. Some folks who ain't willing to risk their lives for anything, who'd rather stay home and let everyone else do their fighting for them."

I knew he was talking about Mr. Morgan.

"Cowards and slackers is what they are," Harley said. "Just plain yellow-bellied cowards."

"Yeah," I heard myself say on my way to the door. "Just plain cowards."

Luther walked partway up the road with me. Before he left to meet Billy, he took hold of my arm and pulled me to a stop.

"Hey, Joe. Come with us. It'll be a good time. Jim's got grasshoppers. . . ."

Just the idea of seeing Jim made something inside me start to boil. Like a kettle ready to start off whistling, I could feel the anger coming up inside me. It didn't matter that he likely wasn't any different than always; it was me, it was a feeling I couldn't stop, one that made my hands go into fists when I saw him, that made my throat go tight when I spoke, my head screaming, "It isn't fair! It isn't fair!"

"I'd better stay home," I said. "There's been lots of chores to do lately."

"That so?" said Luther. "How's that?"

"Just are. I can't go, so quit hounding me about it."

"Well, if you won't come fishing, maybe I'll come by after to say howdy. That all right with you?"

"Sure," I said. "Come by if you want. I'll be there."

Luther showed up after supper with a string of fish for Mama. I have to say it made me jealous to think I'd missed out on such good luck.

THE DAY FINALLY CAME when Luther and Billy and Jim caught up with me. I was just heading over to take a look-see for the box in the field behind Jepson's where Papa said he used to play ball.

"What the heck are you doing, Joe?" Billy asked.

Good question. But I wasn't about to let myself be caught looking like the fool I knew I really was, so I said, "It's a secret."

"Secret? What kind of secret?" Billy walked over to me and spied the shovel. "What are you digging for? Treasure?"

"Sure," I said. "Treasure. Why else would I be digging?"

That did it. Sparks went off in Luther's eyes, and Billy started in on his hopping act.

"What do you mean, treasure?" Jim asked.

"Yeah," said Luther. "There's no treasure around here but that old Spanish gold out somewhere by the ocean."

I had to think fast. "It's a treasure my daddy told me about."

"Where is it?" asked Billy.

"Do I look like I know? I've been digging all over the place trying to find it."

Luther looked puzzled. "Didn't your daddy tell you where it was?"

"If he knew where it was, don't you think he'd have dug it up for himself?"

"What is it?" Jim asked. "Gold? Silver? Diamonds?"

"He never said. I just know there's a treasure buried somewhere around and I'm going to find it."

"I've got a shovel back at my house," Billy said.

"Me too," said Jim. "We're sure to strike it rich!"

"I'll get that old pick of Harley's! That'll dig through anything!"

All three of them took off at a run to get their own personal excavating equipment.

I got the idea this might work pretty well. Four diggers would be better than one, and I decided not to worry about what I'd say when we found the box. For now, I'd let them think anything they wanted.

No news, good or bad, came about Papa, and every day we kept hunting for that box. We went digging three days in a row, putting holes in the ground from one end of the valley to the other. Folks were bound to complain.

"Is that you, Joseph? What are you doing with that shovel? You stay away from my begonias, you hear?"

Mrs. Tilley came at me with her garden rake that day, claiming I was digging up her flower bed, which wasn't true in the least. I might have been nearby—finding a clump of bushes next to her back fence as a likely hiding place—but I never touched her flowers.

Turned out, Mrs. Tilley didn't keep any more silent about me digging up the neighborhood than she did about us swimming naked by the bridge. By the time I got home that afternoon, Mama was smoldering and Aunt Binny was pacing up and down the kitchen ready to wear a hole in the floorboards.

Didn't take Mama any time to light into me. "What in the world have you been up to, Joseph? Mrs. Tilley rang me in a fluster asking how I could allow my boy to go around digging up other people's yards."

"We were just looking for something, Mama," I said, hanging my head like an old hound dog. I felt partly ashamed, partly embarrassed, but mostly just stupid for getting caught.

"Answer me, Joe," Mama said, taking hold of the back of my neck. She only did this when she was truly angry, so I knew not to make up a lie. Aunt Binny sat down at the kitchen table and shook her head.

"We were looking for treasure," I said.

Mama let go and slapped her hands at her sides. "Shame on you," she said. "You boys are too old to be imagining there's gold hidden anywhere around here."

"Sorry, Mama," I said. "We weren't hunting for gold."

"What then?"

"We were hunting for something Papa told me about."

Mama's face drained of color at the mention of Papa. "What is it you're looking for, Joe?"

"Just a cookie tin."

"Cookie tin?" Mama asked. "I know that old thing. Papa had it . . . let me see . . . I think he took it . . ."

"No, Mama. It's something he said he buried a long time ago, to keep it away from his brothers."

Aunt Binny just had to put in her two cents' worth. "I believe that boy needs more work to do," she said. "Keep him occupied and he won't be able to get into trouble."

"He's fine, Binny," Mama said. My sorrowful look must have got to her then, because she came over and gave me a hug. "He's just fine. Making trouble's not in Joe's nature. He's too much like his papa." I hugged Mama back, to apologize and let her know I was grateful for her thinking so highly of me.

Mama made us write letters to Papa again that night.

I wondered why. There was nothing to say. And no one to imagine saying it to. As I wrote, I knew every scratch of my pen was nothing more than a big fat lie.

I wished Mama would understand how I was feeling. I wished she'd understand how it felt to have her always tell me to be like Papa, to "do what your papa would do." I know if it had been me with a wife and three kids, I wouldn't have gone off and gotten lost in some war ten thousand miles away. I never would have left in the first place.

And sure thing I never would have left *me* in charge. How could I take care of Mama? I'd been sure when Papa first left that her sadness couldn't get any worse, but now here it was, tumbling down on us like a big old sorrowful blizzard, and I couldn't help in the least.

But Mama was strong. I found out just how strong the next day.

AUNT BINNY WAS OUT BACK with the girls, sitting on the porch and shelling peas while Alice read and Helen played in the strawberry patch. I was stuck in the kitchen, scraping carrots for the stew Mama was making.

We heard a racket break out on the porch, then Aunt Binny hollering, "Come quick! Come quick!"

Mama was hell-bent out that door like a hurricane, with me close behind.

Binny was hanging on to the railing with peas spilled like hail around her feet and the bowl broken in a million pieces.

Alice was standing next to her, screaming bloody murder.

"What is it?" Mama cried, grabbing hold of Binny to shake her back into this world.

"Look there!" she screamed, pointing past the strawberries to the fence.

I heard a rustling, then a growl, then that old tomcat popped out, all teeth and spit, heading right for Helen.

"Oh, my Lord," Binny said in almost a whisper as she gasped for breath. "Oh, my Lord, it's rabid!"

It wasn't two seconds before Mama started moving, so fast I had to play it over in my mind after it happened.

She lifted her skirt, tucked it into her belt, took all three porch steps in a leap, swooped past the peas into the strawberry patch, scooped Helen up in her arms, and brought her back to the porch, setting her down gentle as anything.

"I'll get Spit," I said. "Maybe this time she'll scare it off."

"Stay put!" Mama shouted louder than I'd ever heard her shout. "Don't let that dog out here! Don't let her out!" With that she grabbed a chunk of firewood from the box by the door, and started after the cat.

"It wants my starfish!" cried Alice.

"It's *my* starfish!" countered Helen.

The cat was squalling up a storm over there, backed up against the fence and frothy at the mouth.

"It'll jump you!" Binny screamed. "Look out there, it'll jump you!"

Anger was leaping out of that old cat's eyes, but it

couldn't match Mama's. She was on a mission, fire burning through her at a creature that had tried to go after her child.

All of a sudden the cat let out a horrifying yowl, as if something was pulling its insides out. And there was our Mama, creeping up on it through the strawberries, slowly . . . slowly . . .

"Mama!" Alice cried. "Mama, come back!"

By now everyone on the porch was making as much racket as that tom, bawling for our poor mama about to get jumped by a crazed rabid cat.

Suddenly Mama lurched forward, two steps, four steps—she charged that cat, her arm raised high over her head. In one heavy swoop she swung that old chunk of wood, knocking the cat sideways into the fence. Mama didn't stop there; two more steps and she was standing over it, beating it as hard as she could until it stopped screaming.

It took Alice much longer.

Poor Aunt Binny was fanning herself like a nervous bird.

"Get that shovel you're so attached to, Joe," Mama said, wiping her forehead with her sleeve as she came up onto the porch. "Bury that poor creature as deep in the ground as you can. Whatever you do, don't touch it, you hear?"

I nodded, still speechless. My mama had killed that cat with her own hands. I'd never seen anything so brave or horrible in all my life.

"You would have done the same," Mama said to me

later that night. "You would have done the same to protect your family."

"But, Mama, you could have been bit," I said, knowing that if she had, only a lot of painful injections would have saved her from that same madness.

"It had to be done, Joe. And it was worth the risk," she said. "It's always worth the risk when you're protecting the ones you love."

"Still mighty brave of you, Mama. Like Papa being brave enough to fight those Germans."

"Yes, I suppose," she said, kissing me on the forehead. "But I think it took a lot more courage for your papa just to leave us all behind."

CHAPTER 17

Sleep's something I usually don't have any trouble with, but that night I couldn't, at least not all the way through. The bedsprings groaned and squeaked. I kept waking up thinking about Mama clubbing things to death, and cats trying to kill my little sisters, and about Papa so far away, maybe dead with all those maimed and mutilated bodies Billy's daddy was carting off the battlefield in his ambulance. I gave up trying to sleep at about four-thirty, got dressed, and walked up the hill to think.

A stiff wind was blowing upriver from the ocean and bringing the sleepy sound of the foghorn with it.

The few lights that were on in the valley glowed fuzzy and pale yellow through the fog. It usually stays up on the hills, but that morning it was smothering the valley, thick like wool and hugging the river.

My brain was foggy too, and I couldn't sort out what to think on. Nothing but worry came into my mind. Every worry about Papa and Mama and me and the girls—they were all mixed up in a jumble in my head. I finally settled on thinking about Jim; about Mr. Morgan and how he hadn't gone off to get himself killed or lost like Papa; about how angry I was at him for that, and at Jim for not losing his daddy.

As I sat there, with my mind so full of bad feelings, it was a wonder I heard what I heard. Part of me wishes now I hadn't, but who can go back and change things? I surely can't.

Fog does funny things to sound. It keeps noises stuck to the ground so they don't float off on the wind. In our valley on foggy nights you could hear a dog bark a mile away, or a horse whinny, or a door slam. If you listened real carefully, you could even hear folks snoring way down in the valley; there were folks who slept outside all summer, thinking that breathing fresh air would keep them from getting tuberculosis.

That morning I could hear the ocean, a faint thundering sound of waves hitting the beach.

And behind that, an odd sort of wailing sound, coming in, and out.

I thought at first someone's baby must be crying. I was curious about it, so I stood up and listened more carefully.

Could I have been imagining things? Maybe I had yowling cats too close on my mind.

But then, there it came again, faint and far away but surely a wailing, coming from the west. From the ocean.

It wasn't crying babies or rabid cats I was thinking about when I ran back home. It was the ocean, the ocean crashing against the rocks on the point, the ocean and the ship I could see in my mind.

I ran upstairs and woke Mama to tell her I thought there'd been a wreck at the beach.

"The horse, Joe," Mama said. "Wake Binny so she can watch the girls, then ride to Reverend Belden's. Get him to ring the bell. I'll follow in the car."

"I'll ride to Luther's too. Maybe his brothers will help."

I bridled the horse and hopped on her, then hightailed it to town and woke up the reverend and his wife.

"There's a wreck at the beach," I said, trying to catch my breath. The reverend yawned and rubbed his eyes, pulling his robe around his nightshirt. "Mama says for you to ring the bell!"

"A wreck? What sort of wreck?"

"I—I—I don't know," I stammered. "I heard screaming. . . ."

"You heard screaming? What kind of screaming?"

Mrs. Belden came to the door. "Don't interrogate the boy, Hiram. For Heaven's sake, go ring that bell. There's no time to waste if there really is a wreck out there." She stepped outside. "Fog's like mud this morning. . . . Hurry up there, go ring that bell! I'll gather blankets. Joe, take our lantern and start banging on doors! I'll try to raise Mabel to telephone as many folks as she can!"

I swung up on that horse and tore over to Luther's. By that time the bell was ringing away, sending its eerie clanging up and down the valley in the foggy dawn air. Harley got to the door first.

"It's a wreck at the beach!" I told him. "I heard wailing from up on the hill."

"You'd better not be fooling now," Harley said as he pulled on his boots.

Ray and Arlo came stumbling downstairs. "Is there a fire?" Ray asked.

"Joe says there's a wreck out at the ocean. Reverend must have believed it because he's ringing the bell."

"Probably a German U-boat," said Arlo, looking wide awake all of a sudden.

By the time I got back outside, just the slightest hint of sunlight was peeking up over the hills at the head of the valley. All up and down the road, lanterns were swaying their weird pale lights in the fog. Jim and Claire and Mr. Morgan were passing by in their truck, and I could see Billy coming on horseback. But I didn't wait for him, didn't wait for Luther.

I didn't even wait for Mama and the Hudson, but cut over the rise, then raced straight down the ocean road ahead of everyone else, the foghorn moaning away in the distance.

It didn't occur to me until then, as I was leading the crowd of helpful worried folks behind me—and, as it turned out, the entire volunteer fire department—that I could have been wrong. What if it wasn't a wreck after all? What if all I'd heard was a baby crying or another deranged cat? I galloped hard, deciding as I rode that if I was wrong I'd just keep riding until I made it to the next county, where I could hide out until everyone got murder off their minds.

But I wasn't wrong. As I rounded the bend at the end of the valley, I could hear it plain as anything. Not wailing, but bloodcurdling screams and the sound of a ship breaking against the rocks. The screaming wasn't human, though. It was horses.

The sea was dark under a gray dawn sky. Wind whipped in gusts, spitting up sand and pebbles to sting my face.

Out there on the ocean, fog swirled over the waves, but I could see the ship, cracked in half and stuck up on the rocks at the point. I wondered if they'd sent an SOS. It was sure too late now. Men were scrambling onto the deck and climbing off onto the rocks.

Then I saw the horses. A whole string of them, tied together out on the deck of that ship.

"Set them loose!" someone on shore was screaming at the men on deck. "Set them loose!"

It was Jim's daddy. He'd hopped out of his truck and was standing knee-deep in the water, shouting at the top of his lungs. I could see why. Tied together like that, those horses would drown for sure if they went into the water. If one horse floundered it would take the others down with it.

"Set them loose!" Mr. Morgan yelled again. But the last man on board didn't hear, or didn't care. He let go of the horses and dove into the sea. Then so did Mr. Morgan.

I don't know if anyone but me and Jim noticed at first. Jim took two steps after his daddy, then turned around and looked at me, pain and fear written all over his face.

"What's he doing?" I yelled over the wind.

"He's going out to get them," said Jim. "He's going out to untie those horses so they don't drown."

The waves took Mr. Morgan under at first and we lost sight of him. Then we saw him, swimming hard through the breakers, out toward the rocks and that crippled ship.

Folks were pulling survivors up onto the beach by now and wrapping them in blankets. Someone had built a big bonfire and it crackled and sputtered, blowing smoke up to mix with the fog.

Mr. Morgan swam hard. Jim took hold of my arm, digging his fingers in.

"He'll be all right," I said, more like a prayer than anything else. "He'll be all right."

We watched Mr. Morgan make his way, and as we did, other folks started to notice too and gathered at the shore to watch.

"Don't tell me that crazy Morgan's gone after those horses," I heard Harley say.

"Lost his mind, that's certain," said someone else.

As Jim and I stood watching, Billy and Luther came over to be with us. Claire left the fire, where she'd been passing out blankets, and ran up behind Jim. She was standing so close to me I could feel her shaking.

Jim's daddy made it to the ship, and between waves we could see him climbing up the side. The horses were going mad, tied like they were, kicking and screaming and bucking. But that didn't stop Mr. Morgan. He started cutting each one of those horses loose and shooing them into the water.

Then the big wave came, the one they say comes one in nine. Or maybe it's eleven, I don't remember; I just know it came big, and crashed against the side of the ship so hard you could hear the hull groan.

"Papa!" Claire screamed.

"Come back!" Jim hollered with all his might. "Leave them, Papa. Come back!"

It was eerie what happened next. The wind and fog were blowing hard off the ocean. There was no way their voices could have carried to Mr. Morgan. But for a moment he turned and looked in our direction, right at Jim and Claire, as if he'd heard them calling for him to come back.

But Mr. Morgan didn't jump off that ship. It lurched and tipped and broke right under him, and he stayed, hanging on to that string of horses, trying to cut the last ones free.

Then it was plain what he was going to do, and my blood ran cold. There wasn't time for him to free each one, so he was going to lead them in, all strung together, past the rocks, through the waves, to the beach.

The ship shook and the horses began spilling into the water, one after the other, tied like that.

Mr. Morgan went after them, fighting the surf as it crashed against the rocks. One of the horses went down.

"It's pulling the others with it!" shouted Luther.

"They're all going to drown!" Billy cried.

Jim just held tight to my arm. Neither of us was

watching the horses anymore. We were watching Mr. Morgan.

He'd managed to grab hold of the rope that tied the horses together, and he was hanging on, bobbing up and down in the waves, trying to cut that rope.

One horse swam free. Then another. There were four horses left when they hit the rocks, slamming hard under the waves and disappearing. Claire cried out, but everyone else on the beach stood still, and quiet, and breathless, just watching in horror.

CHAPTER 18

It was pretty clear cowardice wasn't what kept Mr. Morgan home from the war. I knew that now. The whole town knew it.

Jim's daddy saved sixteen horses that morning. Out of twenty only those last four were lost, tied together with Mr. Morgan still hanging there, his hand clinging to that rope even after he'd died.

Claire had hold of Jim, keeping him back, away from seeing his daddy dead and laid out on the beach.

The reverend and two other men helped lift him into the back of the Morgans' truck, then the reverend climbed in and drove Jim and Claire and their dead daddy back to town.

Most everyone stayed on the beach to dig graves for the drowned horses and to salvage debris. The survivors were taken to the schoolhouse. By noon, newspaper reporters started showing up with cameras.

Once we got home, the girls and I helped Binny cook, fixing food to take over to the schoolhouse and to the Morgan place. Mama went over to Jim's to help wash and dress Mr. Morgan.

I wandered around not knowing what I ought to do, getting in Binny's way and snapping at the girls. Binny finally tired of it and told me I ought to go for a walk and sort out how I was feeling.

As I left she handed me the bundle of letters we'd written to Papa.

I climbed the hill, just like I had that morning, and sat down on my rock the same way I had before I sounded the alarm that killed Mr. Morgan.

Nothing was making any sense. Nothing at all. Papa off lost in France and now Mr. Morgan dead trying to save those horses. I gazed out over the valley, deciding most everything in life was pretty pointless and mighty depressing, and wondering just why so many bad things were coming out of nowhere to change our lives so quick. In a flash—just like Papa'd said.

I wondered about that as I walked back down the hill and into town. And I wondered about other things too, like what the moon is made of, and why the sky is blue, and where Papa might have buried that box . . .

It always seemed to come back to that. I'd dug up so much empty ground I was beginning to think the box must never have existed at all, that Papa had just made it up to tease me.

Passing the waving flags and folks solemnly nodding to me, I wondered what I'd been thinking, wasting my time trying to find it. That stupid box wouldn't bring Papa back any more than the letters I had in my pocket would.

Before I went into Jepson's to mail them, I stopped and sat on the bench outside to think. *"Pvt. Russell Farrington . . ."* was written in Mama's hand. *"Pvt. Russell Farrington,"* in Alice's hand. I thumbed past Helen's to mine on the bottom. *"Pvt. Russell Farrington"*—it read like all the rest, but what was inside was still nothing but a big lie. The outside too, come to think. Who were we kidding, believing these letters wouldn't come back unread? I reached into my pocket and pulled out Papa's knife. It felt cold as stone. I opened it; slipped the blade under the string around the bundle. It made a little snapping noise when I cut through it.

I went into Jepson's and asked him to post the letters from Mama and the girls. He nodded, seeing who they were addressed to. "I'm sure they'll reach him, Joseph. Tell your mother I'm sure they'll reach him."

I thanked him and walked out. As I passed the incinerator at the side of the building, I tossed in the letter I'd written to Papa.

Then I ran all the way back home.

BILLY AND LUTHER were waiting on the porch for me.

"Hey, Joe. Bad do about Jim's daddy, isn't it?" Luther said.

"Yeah," I answered. "Horrible."

"You talk to Jim?" Billy asked.

"No, all his relatives are over there. My mama too. She went to help."

"Want to go fishing?" Luther asked. "Harley and them are still out burying those horses and cleaning up, so it'll be all right."

Fishing seemed as good a way to pass time as anything else, so I said yes.

"I wonder if your brothers'll be any different about Jim, now that his daddy's dead," I said.

Luther looked at me like I'd lost my mind.

As we walked, a dark cloud of depression settled over all of us. Billy started up a conversation about a second bad round of influenza coming our way, and about how he'd read in the paper that the Russians had propped their czar and his family against a wall and shot them. All of us remarked on how terrible that was, but none of it seemed as bad as what was happening in our own lives.

Before we could say more about that, though, Billy's thoughts must have brightened because he went flying off with his arms out wide.

"How's about that treasure?" Luther asked. "You find it yet?"

"Naw, I gave it up. Mama got after me to stop digging around. My daddy was probably mistaken anyhow, or just telling me a whopper."

"Possible," Billy said, zooming in beside us again. "Maybe we could go looking for that gold out at the beach someday. Maybe that's the treasure he was really talking about."

"Sure, I suppose we could," I said. "But I don't think I'm going to want to go near the ocean for a while."

Luther and Billy nodded and we walked on, looking down at our feet. It was going to take us all a long time to get over what had happened out there. I couldn't let myself wonder what it felt like to be Jim, seeing your own daddy die right in front of your eyes like that.

I think that's when I changed my mind about dead being better than missing. Dead might make an end to the wondering, but it sure didn't leave much room for hope.

We fooled around at the river, not doing much fishing but hollering and tossing lots of rocks. It felt good to shout up at the hillside, felt good to shout out the anger I was feeling about all the unfairness in the world and how everything seemed to be going so wrong.

Billy and Luther got into a scrap over who could skip a rock the most times on the water, and finally both ended up in the river with all their clothes on.

Somehow, I didn't feel full of much fun, what with Papa and Mr. Morgan so plain on my mind. I went on skipping rocks. And while I sat there I started wondering again.

Wondering about Papa and the way he'd been that night before he left for the war, talking on so crazy about that box, then just for a second stopping to look at me, almost getting serious before he turned away. It gave me the creeps just then to think about it—it felt almost the same as the look Jim's daddy had given him from out on that ship.

I wonder where . . .

I was thinking about Papa's words, and about his big

hand moving from my shoulder to point out over the valley, then coming back to rest on the rock where he was sitting.

I wonder where I put that . . .

It hit me then, and I knew, just as if he'd told me right out where that box was hidden.

"Got to go!" I shouted at Luther and Billy. They waved but didn't quit pounding on each other and laughing.

I didn't bother going back to the house for the shovel. I ran straight up the hill and started tugging like mad on the rock where Papa always sat. It rolled over easy, as if someone had moved it not so long ago. And the dirt under it moved easy too, in tight little clumps, away from the box that was buried underneath—a rusty old cookie tin with a blue willow pattern, just like Papa'd said.

Sure thing, he'd tricked me. He'd known all along where it was. All his talk and wondering . . . I guess he'd done it on purpose. Maybe so that I'd wonder too, and go looking on my own.

I lifted it out and brushed it off. When I pulled on the lid, it flipped off with a little clang and landed in the grass.

I can't say what I thought I'd find inside, but I figured after he'd gone to so much trouble to coax me into searching for it, it had to be special—holding some particular message for me. A letter, or a book, or a poem, maybe. Something important, like his knife.

But I didn't find anything like that in the box—only a bunch of ordinary stuff. A whistle, a rock, a marble, a bent-up fishhook—just like he'd said. An old ticket stub. A dried flower. Nothing as dumb as prune pits or nerve tablets, but nothing important either. Nothing for me.

But as I looked more closely at what Papa had saved, I began to feel like I was holding all that was left in the world of him and the things he loved.

There was a photo of Mama and the girls and me. The ribbon we'd won last year in the three-legged race. The piece of smooth green glass he'd picked up at the beach on his birthday. And the stick he'd been whittling the night before he went away.

Things he loved. Things he'd left behind.

These were things he'd left for me.

The idea struck me so hard I had to take a breath. But I couldn't keep from crying—the ache inside me for Papa was just too big. I had nothing else to do.

I SAT THERE for a long time after that, just gazing out over the valley like Papa always did, out over our little town, the hills, the river, the ocean—remembering how much he loved it here. How much he loved all of us. And, like Mama'd said, how much courage it must have taken for him to leave everything he loved behind.

I don't know how long I'd been there before I noticed Spit making her way up the hill, following my trail with her nose.

She seemed pleased when she found me, and came

up shyly to sniff the box. She smelled Papa, and it made her tail start wagging like mad.

I reached down and scratched old Spit behind the ear. Nice and easy she rolled over for me and let me scratch her stomach.

We stayed there together for a while longer, until the wind came skirting over the grass and I figured it was time to go.

I closed the box tight, stood up, and tucked it into my shirt.

"Come on, girl," I said. "We'd better get back."

Spit gave out a little yip of approval. Then she hopped up and we chased each other home.

CHAPTER 19

THOUGH I WAS SURE most folks had changed their minds about Mr. Morgan, they weren't all that ready to show it by honoring him at his funeral.

But it was almost comical to watch the folks who did—to see them switch their feelings around to make Jim the celebrity this time; making him famous because he was a hero's son when just yesterday he'd been the son of a coward.

Luther came to the funeral with his mama, but Harley and his other brothers didn't show up. Luther said it was a matter of reputation. I figured he was talking about the tormenting side of their reputation. They'd made such a stink about Mr. Morgan that they were way too committed to thinking poorly of him to change their minds just because he'd died.

But I wondered if it might really be that they were ashamed. Too ashamed to face Jim and look him in the eye. I liked that idea and decided it made them about the biggest cowards in the valley.

I wondered what Papa would say to that.

Even though Andy Marble was killed so young and buried with a flag over his coffin, Mr. Morgan's funeral was by far a sadder affair. But we suffered through, all of us weeping and the reverend doing his best to paint a pretty picture of how Mr. Morgan had died so bravely, saving those horses.

As I stood out in Morgan's field with Mama and the girls, watching Jim, so sad and so strong, there by his daddy's grave with Claire and Mrs. Morgan, I got to thinking how right Mama'd been about bravery—how it wasn't so much fighting Germans or killing cats or saving horses that was courageous. It was choosing to do something you thought was right, no matter what the cost—even if it meant leaving everything you loved behind.

AFTER THE SERVICE, Binny went home to nap, but the rest of us went to the Morgans' house for refreshments and to cheer up the family as much as we could. Just walking into their front room near broke my heart. There was a picture of Mr. Morgan on the mantel now, and the sweet smell of his pipe tobacco was still thick in the air. Jim was mighty broken up, and so was Claire. I have to say she looked truly beautiful when she was sad like that, though I would have traded it for her happiness in a minute.

Folks were talking real soft, saying as many kind things to Mrs. Morgan about her husband as they could, while we all sat on chairs put up against the walls around their front room and ate tea-party sand-wiches and Mrs. Tilley's rhubarb pie.

I was stuck talking to a man named Rice, a fellow who came over from Maxwell to pay his respects.

"I've seen you before, haven't I, son?"

"My name's Joseph Farrington," I said, though I was pretty sure I'd never met him before. "Perhaps you've seen me in town."

"Not likely," he said. "I'm from over Maxwell way. You ever get over to Maxwell?"

"On occasion," I said. "Not often."

"Why, of course! I *do* know you. You're one of those boys who brought those sheep with Harley Thornton, aren't you?"

I had to admit I was, shamed though I might be.

"So, did you get a fair price for them?"

"I reckon."

"I hear Thornton wouldn't bring this man Morgan's sheep."

"No, sir."

"Why is that?"

"He didn't approve of him not going off to the war. But my mama said Mr. Morgan might not have been able to sell them anyway, what with everyone else feel-ing so much the same."

"That so?" Mr. Rice said. "I never knew the man. But saving my horses the way he did . . ." He looked through the window and out over the field where Mr. Morgan's horses were grazing. "Tell you what, Mr. Far-rington. If someone brought those sheep to me, I wouldn't object to giving a fair price. No, sir, wouldn't object at all. If someone gets them there before the train leaves tomorrow afternoon, I'll buy them."

"WE CAN'T DO IT," Billy said when we talked it over later.

"Maybe not, but we might as well try," I said. "What good are they doing anybody if they stay here?"

"What if we lose them?" Luther asked. "What if we make a mess of it like we did the last time?"

"We just won't, is all. We'll just make sure we're concentrating."

Billy was still worried. "What if Harley and them find out?"

"We'll be careful," I said.

Jim was still looking mighty worn out, but he said he was glad of the chance to sell the sheep. "I told my mama about our plan," he said. "She gave us her blessing. She said it was the best she could ask for right now, seeing as how if they don't get bought we won't make it over the winter unless we sell the horses."

"Mr. Rice told me they had to be there tomorrow before the afternoon train."

Jim nodded. "Tomorrow it is then. We'll leave before first light."

IT WAS A LONG WAY from the Morgans' place to ours, but since Binny'd taken the car Mama and the girls and I walked home, none of us talking much, the girls quieter than usual.

With the sun at our backs and our shadows stretching out in front of us, we passed down Main Street. Flags were still waving, the soldier poster was still in Jepson's window, but in that hazy late-summer light everything about the town felt as if it had changed. Calmed and settled somehow. Sad almost, but peaceful too.

I was wondering why that might be when Helen tapped Mama on the arm. "Mama?" she asked. "Is Papa dead, like Mr. Morgan?"

Mama stopped and looked down at Helen. "I don't know, sweetheart," she said, her voice sort of lost and melancholy. "I just don't know."

Helen kept looking up at Mama, as if she expected more of an answer.

Then she looked at me.

I wasn't the least bit sure what I was going to say, but I stepped toward Helen and took her hand.

"Is Papa dead, Joe? Is he dead like Jim's daddy?"

"He's missing," I told her. "That's not the same as dead. It means we don't know where he is. We have to wait until someone finds him."

"Is it like hide-and-seek?" she asked.

"Yes," I said. "Just like hide-and-seek."

Alice moved up beside us. "Papa's brave, isn't he?" she asked, smiling up at Mama.

Mama nodded. "One of the bravest men I know." She glanced my way, that soft, sad look in her eyes.

I reached out and hugged her as the girls skipped on ahead of us.

"Don't worry," I said. "He'll be home soon."

Mama looked at me and smiled most gratefully.

I hugged her again, just to make sure she knew we were all going to be okay.

20

LUTHER AND BILLY SHOWED UP just before five o'clock the next morning. They knocked softly on the door.

"Sun's coming up," Luther said. "We'd better get. Harley and the rest of the boys were out till all hours. If we're lucky they'll likely sleep late."

Mama tiptoed to the door so as not to wake Aunt Binny and the girls. "Your papa would approve, Joe," she whispered, hugging me hard. "I know he'd say you're doing the right thing."

Spit was eager to go to work and trotted happily across the fog-damp grass as we headed out into the morning.

Mrs. Morgan was waiting with Jim on their front porch. "You are all treasures," she said sadly. "So good to us."

Jim kissed her good-bye, then walked over to open the pasture gate.

I sent Spit in to run out the sheep. They came

streaming through like water and headed down the road.

Luther and Billy each took a side. Jim and I split up to work from the rear.

As the sun peeked over the hills, we rode along easy, those bawling sheep spread out in front of us like a woolly blanket. Spit was working fine, zipping around after the stragglers. This time we really were drovers headed for Abilene. This time we were the bosses of the trail, though we didn't talk much since Jim's daddy was still such a big part of our thoughts.

With the sheep behaving and Luther's brothers sleeping off their big night, everything went along fine . . . until we came up on Suicide Curve.

I saw the car first. It was roaring down the road right for us.

"Head them around!" I shouted up the line. "Don't let them split!"

Billy swung his horse about and galloped ahead, trying to turn the sheep.

"That car wants the inside of the turn!" Jim yelled at me. "If we take the outside we'll lose sheep over the edge!"

"Push them up the hill!" I called. "Push them away from the road! They'll scatter, but at least we won't kill any!"

The car was honking away, coming full at us, not noticing in the least that our horses were spooked and ready to buck us off, and that we had sheep running every which way between here and Christmas.

Luther rushed to the back and I sent Spit out to

drive the sheep up the hill; then we all started whooping and hollering and racing along the side of the road until those animals leaped the ditch and took off up the slope above the road.

We made so much dust the car had to slow to near a stop as it passed behind us. Two women leaned out the windows, shaking their fists and cussing in a mighty unladylike fashion. They must have figured we were a bunch of hoodlums pulling a prank, but the way I see it, they ought to have thanked us for saving their lives. That car'd been heading into the curve way too fast.

I was considering what a mess that would have been and wondering if I'd have felt bad if they'd ended up floating facedown in the river below Suicide Curve, when I took a second look at the car and realized just exactly who those two ladies were: Mrs. Brown and Mrs. Cass, coming home from a night of work at the Red Cross. They were the most dedicated volunteer women in the valley, and first and second cousins to Mrs. Tilley in the mouth-to-mouth telegraph service.

I didn't have time to fret over whether they'd roll into town and tell Luther's brothers they'd seen us, because when I turned back to business, sheep were everywhere, running out like a river delta all over the hillside.

Jim and Billy tore up the hill after them, racing their horses so hard you could hear them grunting for breath.

Spit was doing her best to bring the sheep around, but she was only one dog. Right then I calculated we could have used about six.

Jim zipped off to the left to keep them all from running back down toward town, and I stayed put, standing guard in the road, praying they wouldn't head my way too fast and send me flying backward over Suicide Curve.

Pretty soon it became apparent that they weren't going to come my way. In fact, they weren't even going to consider turning back down the hill at all. Those sheep were galloping like mad and making straight for the trees.

Now, letting sheep run is a bad idea for lots of reasons. First, you'll take good weight off them. Second, you're likely to kill a few that might be unsteady on their feet. But worse, when sheep run they go even stupider than they already are. They scatter every which way, imagining a pack of wolves or coyotes is at their heels.

"Tighten them up!" Luther yelled at Billy and Jim. "If we have to chase stragglers we'll be late for the train!" He waved back to me. "Quit daydreaming, Joe! Get on around and keep them out of the woods!"

Luther was starting to sound an awful lot like his brother Harley, but he did have a point. If I could get between the sheep and the trees we might have a chance to turn them.

I called Spit back and sent her out ahead; then I kicked my poor old horse hard to catch up. We might lose a few into the brush, but if we kept them out of the trees and heading uphill in the same direction, we'd be all right.

Spit was barking and I was yelling and waving my

arms like some dumb old bird, doing anything I could think of to scare those fool animals away from the trees, all the time dying at the thought that it might be me who came to lose George Morgan's sheep.

"Bring them this way, Joe!" Jim hollered back at me. "We'll head them over the ridge! We can meet the road on the other side."

Drive them over the top? Oh, well. We didn't really have a choice in the matter. Between Spit's work and mine, most of the sheep were long gone in that direction anyhow.

Going up that hill turned out to be the best idea anyone'd had in a long time. It was nice not to have to worry about any more automobiles coming our way, and we were able to mosey along letting the sheep spread out in front of us. Billy worked the right, Jim the left, and Luther worked the back with me, all of us with our minds on the job and far away from all our recent troubles.

It was approaching eleven o'clock by the time we made it to the top. From there you could see Maxwell in the distance and the whole valley stretched out toward the mountains in the east.

We kicked it up then, working to steer those sheep down onto the road so we'd make it to the train by noon.

Then whoop-de-do, la-de-da! There we were, pushing two hundred head of sheep down onto the road, right down the hill and into Maxwell. And we did it smooth, without a speck of trouble.

We arrived in town just as the noon whistle blew.

When we drove Jim's sheep down Main Street toward the train station, folks came out to line the sidewalk, waving like they'd just heard an armistice had been declared. This time it felt like we were riding in the Fourth of July parade, and I've got to say I felt mighty kingly up there on my horse, reins firmly in my hands, whistling and hooting those sheep forward.

Mr. Rice paid Jim and told us we ought to be proud.

"Did that fine, boys," he said, reaching out to shake hands with each one of us.

After all sorts of pats on the back from the folks in Maxwell and after a big lunch of steaks and cake, we headed home—four worthy heroes, whooping and hollering all the way out of town. I was sure Jim must be feeling comfortable as the head of his family, what with that money from Mr. Rice stashed in his pocket.

It took a while before anybody mentioned Harley and the boys, and then it was Billy who worried first.

"Bet Mrs. Cass told," he said. "Wonder if they'll be waiting for us."

"Probably planning an ambush," said Luther. "Bet they've got a trap set up ahead."

"Hey, maybe they've heard what a swell job we did," Billy said. "Maybe they'll grow new respect for us from being good drovers."

"That doesn't make sense," Jim said. "They'd never change that quick about any of us, but especially not about me."

Jim was right, of course. It wasn't likely Harley or any of the others would ever give themselves a reason to respect us, even if one of us was elected President someday. It just wasn't in their nature.

We took the rest of the ride slow after that, joking and shooting the breeze, but all the time with our eyes on the shadows by the road.

We were almost home when we heard a racket ahead of us around the bend. Then Harley and the boys came walking out of the woods, puffing cigars and laughing together.

Arlo saw us first. "Hey, looky there! It's the Hobby Horse Gang!"

Ray spat, then socked Arlo on the arm. "We were just coming to check on you boys and see if we could rustle a few of your stragglers."

"They're saying you scattered the whole bunch up on Suicide Curve," said Harley.

Arlo started walking toward us. "Where'd you drop them off? In a gully up on the hill somewhere?"

"Ride!" Billy whispered. "Fast, before they get us!"

But Harley took hold of Arlo's arm and stopped him. For a second I thought they were going to walk away.

Then Jim called them back. "I have something for you, Harley," he said.

Luther and I looked at each other, then at Jim. He was pulling out in front of us and pointing that horse of his right smack down the middle of the road toward Harley and the boys.

"What's he doing?" asked Billy.

"Don't know." Luther shook his head.

I sighed. "Appears he's lost his mind."

Even Harley seemed startled. "What do you want?"

We stayed back but kept watch, ready as anything to jump in and rescue Jim if he didn't get his wits about him pretty soon.

"I said I've got something for you." Jim pulled up just inches from Harley and reached into his pocket. Then he yanked out the wad of money and peeled off a handful of bills. "My daddy would have wanted to pay you for helping with the shearing like you did. Twenty dollars ought to take care of it. Or maybe you imagine you deserve a bonus for all the other help you've given me and my family?" Jim leaned down to offer Harley the money.

"I'm not taking your money," Harley said, stepping back from Jim.

"Here, Ray," Jim said, edging his horse toward the other boys. "Then you take it." I thought sure we were going to see Jim's blood spill all over the road any second, but Ray backed up too.

Jim shook his head. Then he held the money out and let it fall to the ground, bill by bill.

"Now, I call that fair and square, don't you?"

Jim didn't wait for Harley to answer. From the look on his face, Harley probably couldn't have spoken anyhow. His eyes were bugging like a run-over toad's.

"We're in for it now," Billy whispered, squirming in his saddle.

I think we were all about nervous enough to wet our pants just then.

But as Jim wheeled his horse around and came prancing back toward us, Harley squashed his cigar in the dirt, leaned down to pick up the money, then walked the far way around us on the other side of the road. Ray and Arlo followed, neither one of them even looking our way.

It took Luther a few minutes to absorb what had happened. He was sitting in his saddle with his mouth open wide enough for a whole swarm of flies to buzz in.

ONE AFTERNOON NOT TOO LONG after that, when we were back in the Pepperwood Grove telling whoppers and reliving Jim's act of bravery, I got to wondering about what made those Thornton boys go around us on the road like they did.

None of us could figure it.

"Maybe they felt sorry for Jim and felt bad about how horrible they'd treated him," Billy said.

We all looked at him, not thinking on this possibility for too long. There was just no way we could talk ourselves into believing it.

"They're yellow-bellied chickens," Luther said, patting Jim on the back. "You scared them off, is all."

We roared about that and tackled Luther, pushing him off the log he was sitting on and rubbing the stubby hairs on his head. Then we wrestled around in the leaves till we were laughing so hard we couldn't breathe. Afterward, we lay there for a while, looking up through the trees at the flickering sky until Billy's thoughts flew off to the war. "Everyone knows America's invincible," he said, sounding real serious. "We've got two hundred warships over there in the fight zone and about a million airplanes."

"Not a million," Luther said.

"Well, maybe not. But we're sure to win the war. You'll see."

"We already won ours," Luther said, laughing again and poking Billy.

What would Papa say about Luther's brothers? I wondered. I guessed he'd wonder too why they finally decided to leave us alone. But I imagined he likely wouldn't call them chicken. Maybe he'd even say they'd done the right thing. After all, we'd gotten the Grove back without any bloodshed, hadn't we?

"What's distracting you, Joe?" Billy asked.

"Just wondering," I said.

"About your daddy?" asked Jim. He spoke soft, sounding a lot like Mr. Morgan.

"Yeah, I suppose," I said. "I'm always wondering about him."

They didn't press—not even Luther, who just gave me a friendly nod and a jab in the side to tell me everything was going to be all right.

I knew word would come about Papa eventually, good or bad, and it would come whether I wondered about him or not. It occurred to me, though, that it was beginning to feel a whole lot more like hoping when it came to the way he was set on my mind. And I suppose it was hoping rather than wondering that I was doing that afternoon when I took out Papa's knife and carved my initials under his in the trunk of that old pepperwood tree.

ACKNOWLEDGMENTS

With a heart full of gratitude, I want to extend sincere thanks to my gentle and gifted editor, Lauri Hornik, whose faith and vision have prodded and guided me on the journey to the end of this book; to my copy editors and proofreaders, Jane Steltenpohl, Barbara Perris, Joanne Mattern, and Amy Van Allen, whose bright pencils have kept me from rewriting history; to author Barbara Glenn, for her honesty, patience, advice, good humor, and friendship; to my sister, Peggy, for the same, and more. And to MGMFB—dear friend, for a lifetime of sharing, no simple words will thank you, but I do.

SUSAN HART LINDQUIST has always lived in California. She received a bachelor's degree from the University of California, Santa Barbara, and is a writing instructor and poet as well as the author of two previous children's novels, *Walking the Rim* and *Wander.* She lives in Walnut Creek with her husband, Paul, their children, Charlie, Madeline, and Sam, and their dog, Jack.